I0740073

Gloria's Gone

A So Cal Novel

Frank Warren

Surfers have a cult of their own making.
Don't readily talk to 'outsiders'
—excepting girls.
Blocking out mainstream society and
rejecting its demands on their time.
Surfing is the primary focus of their lives.
Everything else is of secondary importance;
job, school, cars, even babes.

Bobbie Martinez
California Pro Surfer

Launch yourself on every wave,
find your eternity in each moment.

Henry David Thoreau

She closed the bedroom door soundlessly behind her, tiptoed stealthily down the hallway, through the dark kitchen, and out the backdoor into the balmy summer night.

The station wagon had been readied earlier; its green nose pointed streetward. With an easy pull on the outside handle the overhead garage door swung up quietly.

She eased into the car, leaving the door slightly ajar to avert any noise. Releasing the brake, with the car's engine off and in neutral, she guided the wagon as it rolled slowly and silently down the driveway between the two houses. Keeping the steering wheel steady, she settled into the driver's seat and pulled the car door closed just as they crossed the front sidewalk. "Made it!" she whispered to herself, turning on the ignition and headlights, stepping on the gas at last. No note left as to why she had left—let him figure it out.

Alongside the prone figure, a yellowed, splotchy balsawood surfboard lay like an enlarged, flattened-out, ripe banana. The immobile surfer's head, with its shock of bleached out, shaggy, over-the-ears hair, was resting on a pilfered L.A. Biltmore Hotel pool towel. "Charging the batteries" was the So Cal terminology for his comatose, reptilian-like sunning position.

Steve Lund had been bodysurfing the south side of Huntington Pier's break since the age of twelve, some eight summers distant, and graduated to surfboarding some years ago.

His cherished and timeworn surfboard was a pre-war Pete Peterson with no logo, hand shaped by Pete from a balsa blank and sandwiched with redwood. The redwood rails, tip and skeg were dinged up, but intact. A heavy ten-sixer built as a big wave gun.

It had been a thirty-buck steal at a Santa Monica garage sale three years ago. The old dame selling her stuff didn't know anything about the skuzzy old log left in her garage by her long-gone, longhaired renter. "He went to Hawaii one winter and never came back or wrote," she explained.

The striped, cream and russet-colored plank weighed in at sixty pounds, was yellowed with age, and thickly coated with countless layers of Val Spar Marine Varnish. The paraffin coating the big board's topside deck to the rails was encrusted with rough beach sand. "Kinda like riding a giant sanding block," Steve always remarked when asked how it rode. Though a bastard to lug across a broad expanse of hot white beach while barefooted, the ancient Peterson was worth the effort when it came time to ride the wintertime double-overhead storm surf at Huntington Bluffs and the Southside peaks that slapped the underside of the Huntington Beach Pier. Since he couldn't afford a quiver of seasonal sticks he'd settled for "The Log," as he called it.

An early morning ride at Huntington was Steve's idea of the perfect place to be on the coast. By noon, the lithe young surfer lay motionless, face down, his feet shoved under the sand. He resembled a barkentine's shipwreck survivor, clad only in faded and frayed blue twill trunks. Deeply summer tanned and solidly built, a conspicuous pink four-inch scar, high on the right shoulder, marred his torso. The mark resembled a recent, and deep, slash from a sabre, but was actually a skeg slice by an errant board that had taken fifteen stitches to close. No surfing at all for three weeks and then three more to heal up completely. Six whole weeks of surfing time lost. Bummer.

A dark shadow suddenly blocked the bright sun from the prone surfer's face. He sensed a presence without opening his eyes.

"Steve? Steve Lund?" an unfamiliar, masculine, vaguely European-sounding voice called out. "I need your help."

The young surfer did a slow pushup off the sand and rocked back to a kneeling position, shaking his head from side to side to dispel the daydream of riding twenty-foot humpers rolling in from the Hawaiian Islands.

Squinting into the bright beach glare, Steve looked up sideways at the unfamiliar middle-aged man standing next to him. The guy wore steel-rimmed spectacles and was dressed in a short-sleeved blue chambray shirt with a ballpoint pen clipped into the breast pocket, pressed khaki pants, and brown penny-loafers. Maybe not an officer of the law but definitely a square, clearly out of place standing, fully street dressed, in the middle of a hot beach.

"Yeah, I'm Steve," the tanned and sand-covered boarder replied cautiously. "What kind of help would that be, Mister?"

"I'm Dieter Hess. Gloria's father," announced the man in a breaking voice. "She's been missing nearly a week. I don't know what happened or what to do next. The Long Beach Police don't have one goddamned clue or any answers for me... When was the last you saw Gloria at the beach, son? She was coming down here to surf on her new surfboard nearly every day this summer, ever since graduating from Wilson High. Then she left home, sometime late last Sunday night. Took her car, her surfboard, and some clothes. Just gone. Walked out and vanished."

"I haven't seen Gloria here, or anywhere else, since last Saturday afternoon," said Steve matter-of-factly. "I heard about her disappearance on Tuesday. Her girlfriend Darlene phoned and told me about it. Bad news travels fast, I guess. She was mystified too."

"I need to hire a surfer to search for my missing daughter. Her girlfriends told me where to find you. Gloria's disappearance is driving me crazy. I can't sleep or eat; I can't do a decent job at work. Being a competent tool and die machinist takes lots of concentration. I can't just quit my job and go off searching for her. And obviously, I'm not cut out for detective work," Hess sighed with a tone of desperation. "I think the most likely place she might be is somewhere on the south coast... some beach town or other. Maybe she just got bored or angry with me and wanted to get away for a while. I need to talk to her. I just want to know she is OK, and not in any big trouble... or pregnant.

"Please. She's all I have now and I am willing to pay well for your time. Thirty days is all I'm asking of you. What do you do all summer long, besides go to the beach and surf?" asked Hess as he squatted down to eye level, confronting Steve. "Do you have a job?" The stranger's red-rimmed eyes looked tired, the face haggard.

"Yeah, man, I have a job. My own delivery service. Leaves my days free to surf." Steve gazed off toward the breakers, then back at Hess. "What does all this have to do with me, anyway? I know Gloria only slightly. Never dated her. She's a nice looking girl, sure, but pretty sassy and snotty, in my opinion. No offense," Steve added, apologetically.

"You don't understand why I'm here to see you. She's not going to be found by a detective agency or the police. They wouldn't get anywhere questioning hardcore surfers and beach bums. You know the surfer crowd, a close-knit bunch of anarchists and hedonists, according to what Gloria has told me. I don't know why she cares so much about surfing. It will take one of your own kind to pry any information about her disappearance from those mavericks, even for a price. No disrespect to you personally, Steve."

Mr. Hess held his hand up and added, "I'm not really angry with my daughter. I never struck her, except for a few deserved swats on the behind, years ago. She's a good girl, but I keep a tight rein on her activities and nights out. Did you know that her mother, Grace, died two years ago? It has been a rough couple of years for Gloria, but she seemed to be recovering under the care of her psychologist.

Why she took off without a word or a note is beyond me. If she's pregnant, or if she's in some other kind of trouble, we can work that out between us."

"Why come to me, asking me to track down your wayward daughter. It's doubtful she's in any great danger. And I'm not Sam Spade, Private Eye. I'm just a twenty-two-year-old surfer. Nothing real special about me. I'm not about to take off on some goofy Gloria wild-goose chase. Sorry. And I'm not about to shut down my business for you or anyone else. No thanks!"

"I called around among her girlfriends to find out who they thought would be the most logical person to search the beach towns, a surfer to help me find my daughter. Your name was mentioned as my best option. I want you to check around among the surfer crowd up and down the coast. Someone's bound to spot Gloria and her surfboard, or recognize her station wagon. I'll put up a cash reward for information leading to her whereabouts. I know you can find my daughter sooner than anyone else. I need your help, Steve. Will you do it?"

Steve realized Hess was right: a professional private detective sniffing around the surfing beaches would stick out like a white polar bear in Hawaii, would learn zip, *nada*, and be sent off on a fool's errand, for laughs.

He closed his eyes, still kneeling on the sand, and did not answer Mr. Hess for some moments. Finally, he met Mr. Hess's questioning gaze and answered.

"Gloria could be anywhere from Santa Barbara to San Diego if she went to hang out near a surfing beach. Maybe your beach town hideout theory is bogus and she went up to Nor Cal or Oregon. Maybe you'll get a postcard someday from her from Hawaii. I'm not really cut out for detective work, Mister. I'm strictly a surfer and biker, probably too flakey and hedonistic to be of much use to you.

"Besides, private detectives are licensed by the state. I'm not. Don't plan to ever be. You can't legally employ me as some bounty hunter guy. I could take some cash for expenses for doing some snooping around for you, and a finder's fee if I come up with something that leads to Gloria's being found, but I couldn't be working for you, *comprendo*? No written reports, no checking in when there is nothing much to say."

"You certainly have a rather strange and unorthodox way of doing business, Mr. Lund," the stranger said.

"That's 'cause I'm an unorthodox guy, at least according to your conventional world. In my small world, hedonists are the norm and unorthodox is our standard lifestyle."

"What kind of lifestyle do you live? Why did Gloria's girlfriends recommend you?"

"I cruise the SoCal beaches and pick up news, good and bad, from my surfing crowd. You haf'ta water the vines before harvesting the grapes of gossip. Finding out where and when the surf is up and where it's flat. Get my drift?

"I might be open to an attractive offer with no strings, but, as I said, I don't keep track of my time or expenses for anyone. Just being a surfer and running my delivery service at night suits me just fine. No boss and no clock to punch."

"Exactly what kind of delivery service do you have?"

"Night-time package delivery, NQA Messenger. Just me an' my motor, a Matchless 500. Deliver a package anywhere in LA from 9 PM to 2 AM with No Questions Asked, that's my specialty. I'm not keen on dumping my clients cold turkey for you or anyone else. Just happy, doin' what I'm doin'."

"Maybe that is something we can work around," said Hess.

"If I did decide to tear off on my steed to rescue Princess Gloria, I would first have to think your proposition over. If I did find her what's the payoff—and what is it if I don't? I'm a mercenary kind of guy. You should realize that up front."

"How about a five-thousand-dollar finder's fee if you locate Gloria within a month, plus expenses to five hundred—and you keep a thousand dollars if you... if you can't find her? The five hundred up front, to start. That's about as much as I can afford to pay."

"Sure you can come up with all that cash if I do say OK? If you can't, you're just wasting my time here, talking bullshit."

"I can handle the money part and give you the five hundred dollars in cash when you agree to accept my offer. How soon could you start? The sooner the better."

"Give me two days. One to think this over and another to arrange for my bike jockey replacement... if we have a deal, that is. I'll call you tomorrow evening with my yes or no."

Getting to his feet, Steve stooped down to tuck his Peterson and Biltmore beach towel under his right arm. "Right now, I'm as clueless as you are about where Gloria may be hanging out. Might as well get going and head back to Long Beach." He led the way to the parking lot at the highway where they shook hands and exchanged phone numbers.

"Thank you, Mr. Lund. I'll be expecting your call tomorrow," said Mr. Hess.

"The thanks may be premature, Mr. Hess, but I will call," said Steve.

The hardcore surfer knew more about Gloria Hess than he had let on. Brown doe eyes and short, auburn hair with a few sun streaks framed her rather narrow face and small mouth. Somewhat slim. She moved with tentativeness on long slender legs like a doe in a glen, Steve thought. Gloria always seemed on edge, and never looked quite comfortable talking to new acquaintances. He doubted she'd be at ease in a beach party crowd or at a dance. Not the good-time party-time girl with her strict dad ruling the roost. Gloria had dated a surfing buddy of his a few times but he'd been chased off by Mr. Hess.

Her animalistic nervousness caused Steve to feel edgy when they had occasionally talked on the beach at Huntington. Maybe she was more relaxed while bumming around with her trio of girlfriends. The conversations she had with him on the beach had dealt mostly with surfing technique. Steve had shown her some basics such as positioning herself on the surfboard and timing the incoming wave.

"Surfing's like learning to ride a bike," he'd explained. "Looks easy enough when you're watching someone else do it. It's mostly just balance and timing. You'll have to do it all alone, without training wheels. Learning to surf is also a solo event. For starters, keep your weight centered over your board and arms out to the side for balance. Stroke hard and deep when on your knees. Don't just paddle with your hands like you are sitting in a canoe or kayak. You gotta be in sync with the surge of the incoming wave and go with it. Got that?"

That was the core of his surfing philosophy and liquid lifestyle. She had smiled and nodded at Steve's indoctrination to surfing. He wasn't sure if she got it all—or any of it.

He watched from the shore as Gloria was out trying to catch a three-footer and laughed to himself when she pearled her new Velzy surfboard straight in. It reminded him of a kid standing up alone at the center of a teeter-totter. When a surfer steps up beyond the center point, the surfboard tip drops down. Same concept for a teeter-totter except on a surfboard the surfer has to center-balance on a liquid surface.

As he watched Gloria's off-balance gymnastics, she finally managed to remain standing on a broken wave for about four or five seconds. No one can explain to you exactly how to surf; you just go out and try until the "knack" connects with your brain.

At home that evening in Lakewood, Steve made some calls to a few seldom-employed buddies and connected with Bill Bristow, a fellow biker, who was eager to take a thirty-day delivery job at a hundred per week. Bill rode his Italian Bultaco 250cc cycle with abandon and assured Steve he could handle the work, "No sweat."

"We'll see about that 'no sweat' tomorrow night. We ride together starting at nine and see how it goes," said Steve.

Steve had started up NQA Messenger to fulfill a specific need for a certain group of individuals in the L.A. environs. The money was great and not much overhead, plus no reportable income to the IRS.

He had owned Quicksilver, his Matchless G80 bike, for about a year. The ride had been previously owned by an acquaintance, Larry Saunders, who'd been in that late teens stage of life when one considers oneself immortal and invincible. He wasn't.

One spring evening at dusk, Larry was wheeling fast down sinuous Carbon Canyon in Orange County when a doe decided to spring across the road, right in front of him, to meet her lover boy waiting on the other side. The Matchless drilled Bambi's mom dead center. Larry was catapulted over the bars at sixty per. DOA for both. The bike wasn't a total loss but needed major front-end work plus a new tire and wheel. The distraught parents just wanted the evil bike gone. Now. Steve paid them two hundred to haul the Matchless away and out of their sight and lives. Steve, with the help of Larry's dad, shoved and pushed the basket case bike, which weighed almost four-hundred pounds, up a slick plywood ramp and into the back of his van.

He drove directly to Blackie Reeves's Cycle Shop in North Long Beach to unload his wounded steed. Blackie, at age thirty-three, was the size of a wiry jockey. He'd been in more accidents and broken more bones in dirt track motorcycle racing than most steeplechase jockeys had in their careers.

Blackie had been "fixin' bikes" for almost twenty years and was the best in So Cal. "Lucky it wasn't you, Steve," said Blackie when he saw the clot of deer hair and dried blood on the bike.

"I'm still ahead of the Three-seconds Rule, Blackie," answered Steve. "Three seconds this side or the other of death! So, after restoring its front-end damage to factory specs, I want you to modify this banged-up Brit for the streets. Replace the spring seat with an Ariel elongated saddle and change the handlebars to clip-ons. That'll give me a lower profile and less wind resistance."

"Sounds good so far. Let's modify the engine to boost the horses. I'll mill the head to increase the compression to 6.5:1 and polish the OHV seats. I can also bore your one lunger out to 520ccs and fit it with a race exhaust so it'll breathe better. A little noisier, but legal. It'll scamper like a scalded cat. No one'll catch ya!" said the middle-aged biker, scratching his black stubbled whiskers.

"That's exactly what I need, Blackie. A machine that neither the fuzz nor anybody else can catch, and able to hold the road like a panther on your back. Take your time and do it right; there's no big rush," said Steve.

The 1950 Matchless G80 was a twin for the AJS, except for the signage and placement of the single Amal carburetor and the magneto. Factory rated at 497cc (30.3 cu. In.) and 23 horses @ 5,400 RPM, the top speed was 84 MPH. Not any longer!

On a hot and windless late spring Saturday morning Steve and Blackie hauled the modified, but still untested, Matchless out to the Mojave Dry Lake, strapped securely into the bed of Blackie's hot '40 Ford pickup. They planned to run the bike through the So Cal hotrod speed trap on the alkali flats. Blackie had fueled Quicksilver up with high-test aviation gas for maximum speed at the trial runs.

Steve wore Blackie's full-face motorcycle helmet—no windscreen for the run—and for the first test run mile through the traps they clocked 101 MPH.

"Let's not push our luck any further, Steve," said the alkali-covered Blackie. "We broke one hundred and your tuned machine is more than ready for the streets."

"That it is, Blackie, thanks to you. Let's head on home," replied Steve.

The 1950 Matchless, modified to 520ccs was now all black and chrome. Three-inch foot pegs were welded to the frame just forward of the rear axle. This put the iron-horse rider in a low center of gravity and reduced the wind resistance.

A narrowed fuel tank was fabricated so the bike jockey's knees could squeeze the tank tightly on sharp turns and curves at high speeds. Man and machine welded into one unit of flesh and steel and ridden jockey style: tight, low, and fast.

The road bike perfectly matched his night riding needs. Harley Hogs were too heavy and sluggish for this kind of "catch the fox" job; German BMW road bikes were designed for the Autobahn and highways, not for narrow beach city streets and twisting county roads. The Brit-built Quicksilver now had just the right "feel" on LA's urban and beach town streets; the machine was equally at home zooming up the twisty narrow canyons of the surrounding foothills.

Big bore, single cylinder, two-stroke engines carried the nickname 'Thumper.' The loping resonance of the engine at idle speed resulted in the Matchless and AJS 500cc bikes being tagged with that distinctive moniker. Cranking up Quicksilver was like stirring a hornet's nest with a stick. Hop on, give a twist of the wrist to the throttle, hang on tight, and GO!

Steve's nighttime hours coincided with those of his nameless night owl clientele, whomever they may be. He didn't know and didn't care to know what the sealed envelopes and packages contained, likewise he didn't ask from and to what person. "Betta fo' yo' health dat ya' don't know jack," one heavy-duty regular client told him.

The package goods—some with the familiar aroma of pot—were delivered anywhere in the So Cal beach cities area within two hours or less, usually a half-hour. Cash up front—no delivery receipt necessary. Steve never lost nor opened a client's package.

A five-spot per pickup added up to half a C note average for an evening's work. Two-fifty per week was worth the minimal risk. Nobody Steve knew was knocking down a grand a month doing a legit job for The Man. Quicksilver sported black leather saddlebags over the rear fender for its packages. Steve and his bike were a black and chrome speed demon ghosting through the night.

On numerous nighttime occasions, the motorized police, especially the Long Beach PD blues on their black and white Harley Hogs, had gone mad in fruitless hot pursuit—sirens wailing and red lights flashing—after the quicker and always elusive Quicksilver and its jockey.

CHP roadblocks set up to snare drunk drivers were easy enough to spot up the road at night and simple to avoid on a bike by whipping a quick U or turning up a through side street. It was a certainty that there would be an unpleasant encounter, with dire consequences, at a roadblock stop. His Matchless was unstoppable on the streets at night so roadblocks didn't concern the scooter jockey at all.

Steve wore a full set of black leathers with black biker boots and matching gloves while working. He topped his gear off with his "lucky" black wool watch cap. Cop-style Ray-Bans with yellow lenses seemed to enhance his night vision on the dark streets, and also kept the bugs out of his eyes.

There had been only one occasion so far to lay Quicksilver down on the street, although there had been some hairy close calls. Hazard pay there was not. "You can't always beat the Three-seconds Rule," he always said, "but you can hope to avoid the deadly TSR by staying alert, focused, and always ready to react defensively. Ride your machine like you are invisible. Don't ever assume the other guy sees you. The left-turn blinker on just means it's on."

The Three-seconds Rule is always ticking when riding the mean streets of So Cal at night. Three seconds earlier—or later—into an intersection can be fatal to a hot iron-horse jockey tangling with inattentive and drunk drivers. "Just didn't see 'em, Ossifer!" equals a mangled biker.

Late one gloomy and misty Friday night, March 13 to be exact, a contractor's errant truck was "beating" a yellow-turning-red traffic light on Lakewood Boulevard after its bearded and bleary-eyed driver had tossed down more than a few pints at his way-home pub.

Steve was concurrently timing the green light signal from South Street, the cross street. The Three-seconds Rule was in effect.

'Oh, fuck!" Steve cursed as his heavy Matchless braked, fishtailed, and slid to the right on the oil-sheened, shiny asphalt roadway.

He had no other options but to lay Quicksilver down on its left side, bike and biker skidding just beneath the massive, steel rear bumper of RJ Construction's one-ton Ford flatbed truck. "RJ" didn't slow down, stop, or look back, oblivious to the damage caused, Country music blared out of the truck's window.

The black and chrome motorcycle skittered wheels first into the rain-filled gutter, banged hard into the concrete curb with its jockey still in the saddle, and came to an abrupt jarring stop.

That goddamn Three-seconds Rule damn near did me in on Friday the Thirteenth! Steve swore as he shoved the heavy Matchless up and off of his left leg. Didn't feel as if he had any broken bones and he didn't see any major damage to Quicksilver. The left saddlebag was ripped open, and his body leathers and boot had taken a scouring during his roadway slide. The heavy, leather biker skins had literally saved his tender ass.

A small pool of leaked gasoline and crankcase oil glistened purple and gold on the wet street under the intersection lights. The fuel tank was gouged, scraped down to base metal. The entire machine would need to be thoroughly cleaned and checked over, costing a few Franklins.

No police had arrived on the scene, so no accident report needed to be dealt with or questions answered. Just as well since the contractor's truck was long gone. No LBPD hassle needed or time wasted on them.

Steve pushed the bike slowly into the Mobile Oil station on the corner and called Bettie's Answering Service—cancelling the rest of the night's pickup and delivery calls. Bettie told him to "watch where you are going." He called Blackie at home and the old dirt biker agreed to swing over to retrieve the bike and its owner. Quicksilver would be back in motorcycle rehab for a week, and meanwhile Blackie would lend him a Honda 250cc rice rocket.

What was white, black, purple, and stiff the next day? Steve's entire body.

Thursday afternoon, Steve drove his panel truck up to Downey and discussed the proposition for Gloria's search with his Uncle Bert, who'd retired ten years ago, at age fifty-six, from the LAPD's vice and missing persons department. The ex-cop still wore his salt-and-pepper hair in a police-style crew cut, and he was still heavy set—rock solid. If anyone accidently bumped into him, they would just bounce off, as if they had hit a guardrail in their car on the freeway.

Uncle Bert briefed the neophyte bounty hunter on the basics in planning the Gloria search. The retired detective donated his thirty-plus years of expertise to his nephew in a long discussion over several cold cans of PBR out in Bert's backyard patio.

Bert no longer moved around too quickly after he'd taken a .38 slug in the right hip while on a midnight shift on Hollywood Boulevard. The pimp in the maroon velvet outfit who'd pulled the trigger during a vice bust was now underground at Forest Lawn and wasn't moving at all. Bert had put him there with one .38 magnum load, chest centered. "Bull's-eye Day" was grizzled Uncle Bert's apt description of his abrupt retirement from LAPD Vice.

"Don't carry a gun. Have a plan and map out your areas of search. A fat reward is always good— make it a grand, cash—and be sure to grease some palms along the way... Everyone loves cash, and it gets results. Call me anytime. I've had twenty years in the lost and lowlife people business, you know. And these days I'm not doing too much anyway," was the sage cop's parting advice.

Later that afternoon, Steve phoned Mr. Hess at the machine shop. He was relieved to hear Steve could begin his search for Gloria right away. The two agreed to meet that night at eight to discuss plans.

During the next thirty days, Steve planned to check out five California coastal counties; some were larger than small European countries. It might wind up being a short search or an entirely fruitless month with no sign of Steve's prey.

The majority of hardcore So Cal boarders lived at or near their favorite surfing beaches. Steve would need to spend some time making phone calls to his local pals who in turn had friends in the northern and southern beach towns from Santa Barb to Diego.

With these intros, Steve could scooch into the local crowd without raising too many hackles. Generosity with six-packs of tasty Schlitz, and a few baggies of prime weed thrown in for good measure, would start most surfer tongues wagging. The incentive of a major wad of cash would also keep their eyes wide for Gloria and the Velzy.

Mr. Hess was correct in assuming the raucous and nonchalant beach crowd wouldn't open up to Outsiders, Fuzz, or Flatland Freddies. Boarders didn't trust those types—for good reason. An unknown guy could be a Narc, easy, pretending to be a surfer dude or student, but looking to do a drug bust involving one of various entrapment schemes. Never sell or give any grass or dope to a stranger was the wary surfer's rule. Steve knew a few dumbasses, now ex-surfers, who were doing a stretch in the gray-bar hotel for breaking The Rule.

By Friday night, Gloria had been missing for five days without a trace or word from her to anyone. Mr. Hess told Steve that she'd taken a sport bag of summer clothes, two Catalina swimsuits, a couple of beach towels, and some cosmetics. Nothing else that he knew of, at least. She had no checking account, only a bank savings passbook with a couple of hundred in it. Hess told Steve he would call the bank on Monday, but suspected the cash was gone now. Not much else missing from home, except Fred, a caramel-colored teddy with one brown eye and tattered fur coat. Of course, her new Velzy surfboard was long gone as well.

Plain Jane had disappeared along with Gloria. The pea-green, '48 Chevy station wagon had been her high school graduation present. "PJ" had once been her mother's car and had been stored on blocks in their garage for two years before becoming Gloria's. There were hundreds of ubiquitous, green Chevy wagons on California's roads, so that fact wasn't going to help much in the search. That useless 'information' was like asking a stoned-out surfer on the beach, "Seen any brown dogs running loose around here lately?"

Dieter Hess said he'd called the Long Beach Police Department the following Monday morning to report his daughter was missing from home and that he had last seen her about 10:30 Sunday night. A pair of Mutt and Jeff officers arrived at the Hess residence on upper Ximeno in their black and white Ford sedan about 11:30 AM Monday morning. The tall and lanky patrolman, Jeff, came into the front room to fill out the routine Missing Persons Report while Mutt, the short, rotund one, peered leisurely around the perimeter of the house and poked aimlessly through the Hess garage's jumble of storage boxes.

Jeff, the beanpole cop, glanced briefly in Gloria's bedroom, took her high school graduation photograph with him, and jotted down her physical description. He wrote down Plain Jane's CA license plate number and left a police business card with her assigned case number penciled in. That was about all Mr. Dieter Hess, ordinary Joe Blow, received for his city tax dollar. Runaway and missing teens were an everyday, humdrum occurrence to the LBPD. A missing girl was not even a newsworthy item for the local *Long Beach Press Telegram*—unless her daddy was rich or famous. Mr. Dieter Hess was neither. With no evidence of a crime, Hess was basically told, in so many words, not to expect much. "Most likely she'll turn up when her cash runs out," was Jeff the cop's parting words.

The rookie bounty hunter knew that if anyone wanted to drop out—get lost—there were plenty of scuzzy beach towns on the So Cal coast where it would be easy enough to do. The most likely locale to disappear into was the one with the most people in it, according to Uncle Bert. Easy to get lost in a crowd, as the truism goes. That locale would be the fifteen-mile stretch of aging beachfront from Redondo to Santa Monica. A myriad of benign, stucco apartment buildings and sleazy motels, all needing minimum-wage women to clean up and scrub off some stranger's residue and crap, dotted the strip.

The abundant and invisible motel maid and house cleaner jobs required no references or ID. That sort of semi-temp employment generally paid by the week, Friday afternoon, in cash. Show up on time, do the shitwork, don't gripe or steal stuff, and stay cool to the horny boss man. Easy as that to hide out—no questions asked.

Waitressing was another possibility that Steve considered, but those jobs had a higher visibility factor for a good-looking babe who was trying to remain anonymous and incognito. He also realized there wouldn't be enough time to check out all the swing shifts in every café and hash house on the So Cal coast in thirty days, or even in six months.

On Friday evening at eight, the evening still warm but beginning to cool, Steve drove in his old panel truck to the Hess home, located in a Midwest Iowa look-a-like residential neighborhood. The single-story home was built in the 1920's Craftsman bungalow style with a wide veranda. The stark-white stucco, edged with black trim, looked a little out of the ordinary. The Bermuda grass front lawn was slowly being sucked dry by the two towering date palms straddling the front walk. The twin trees swayed high above the house on their shaved and naked brown trunks.

Dieter Hess anxiously ushered his newly hired investigator of missing daughters into the bare entryway and through the sparsely furnished living room. They sat down on a pair of chrome and white vinyl chairs at the white Formica-topped table in the spotless white and black themed kitchen. A matching set of shiny chrome canisters was carefully arranged on the black and white tiled kitchen counter, the five cans arranged one inch apart. No dishes, no towels, no toaster in sight. Spotless. This guy has to be a Mr. Tight-ass, no-nonsense engineering type, thought Steve. Definitely an Eisenhower guy. No wonder she hauled ass out of here. Gloria's father couldn't come up with the slightest explanation of why, or where, she might have skipped out on him. Steve had now guessed the why.

"No unusual disagreements or row with me," Mr. Hess flatly stated. "No steady boyfriend to elope or run off with either, thank God!"

Grace Hess, Gloria's mother, had died abruptly from a brain aneurysm two-and-a-half years ago. Gloria came home from school and found her, stone cold, sprawled on the kitchen floor with a coffee mug still clutched tightly in her hand.

"Gloria has only recently been recovering from her moods of depression over the enormous shock of her mother's sudden death. My daughter has been seeing a psychiatrist for some time now," explained Mr. Hess in his matter-of-fact voice.

Steve jotted down Dr. Helen Grayson's office phone number. Better try and get Gloria's version of her mother's sudden death and the aftermath trauma from her shrink. Monday, before taking off on this quest, Steve planned to call and set an appointment to see this neurosis-mender in person. Mr. Hess said Dr. Grayson knew about Gloria's disappearance. He hadn't forgotten to call her, he said, though he'd suspected, and was proved correct, that she would not be particularly helpful. The news was a shock to the mind doctor too. Steve told Hess that he would phone Dr. Grayson himself on Monday.

The neophyte detective laid out his proposed plan, as outlined by Uncle Bert. Steve would start his search of the coast starting just north of Santa Barbara and then move his way south toward the San Diego area.

A more thorough search of the Santa Monica-Redondo Beach area would probably wind up the month. "Just like casting a net," explained Steve. Meanwhile, Mr. Hess would scan the local papers daily for any ads or accidents that might show any sign of her and call the LBPD for any possible news, keeping a particular lookout for any classifieds offering a Velzy surfboard for sale or a '48 Chevy station wagon.

Two hundred and fifty photo-fliers with a picture of Gloria in a Catalina swimsuit, holding her Velzy board, would be rush ordered by Steve for Monday. MISSING in large block letters just above her photo, her name and physical characteristics printed at the bottom: five-foot five, one hundred and ten pounds, brown eyes, short, light brown hair, small mole on her chin. Descriptions of the station wagon and the yellow Velzy would also be listed. Finally, the number of where to call collect if she was seen and the $1,000 Reward for Information were posted prominently at the top of the fliers.

Dieter Hess's eyes widened as he took a deep breath at the $1,000. But Steve explained the mercenary hook of the reward money was a key factor for success. "You won't be out that extra grand if she's not found, or if I find her without anyone's help," explained Steve.

"Here is a list of Gloria's closest friends and her address book. I'm pretty sure she doesn't have a steady boyfriend, but her girlfriends would surely know that for sure," mentioned Mr. Hess as he handed over the list and her small address book.

One of Steve's buddies had dated Gloria a few times and Steve knew the guy was now living up in Malibu. That connection would be worth checking out. There was also great surfing up there to look forward to. The Gloria search was not a 24/7 job to Steve.

"I want to look over her bedroom. There may be something in there that may help us." Mr. Hess showed him the way, opened her bedroom door, and stepped aside. The messy room hadn't been touched since Sunday night, the bed still unmade, according to her father.

"I don't go in there," he mumbled.

Steve sifted through school notebooks and scattered papers. He poked through the clothes that were still randomly tossed about the room, then rooted around in the closet without finding anything of interest. He left in place a dog-eared paperback, *Your Body and Sexuality*, nestled in the bottom drawer of the dresser, but took the notebook page with handwritten phone numbers that he found tucked inside the book, to check against those listed in her address book. He quickly noticed that one of the phone numbers on the page was his. He pocketed the paper, flipped the light off, and walked back into the black and white kitchen where Mr. Hess sat, waiting quietly, hands folded on the empty white table.

"Find anything?"

"Nothing of any help."

Mr. Hess handed his searcher five hundred dollars in fifties, the agreed upon advance to get the search underway, and Steve gave him a notepad receipt for the cash, no mention of what for.

"Let me know if and when you need more," he told Steve.

"I'll let you know. This'll be fine for now. Remember, this search was your idea, Mr. Hess, not mine, so if at any time at all you want to call it off, just tell me. Let's both keep a positive attitude. Jot down anything you read, or hear, that may be a possible lead and I'll check it out. There's no such thing as an insignificant lead. OK? I'm going to interview your neighbors about the weekend and night of Gloria's disappearance. Tell me about the people who live next door."

"On the right side is Mrs. Epstein, a widow who lives alone. On the left, to the north, are Brian and Roxanne Brandon, a young couple with no children. I don't know any of the others on this street by name. Gloria did baby-sit a few times for the people across the street in the yellow house, Jane something," recalled Mr. Hess.

"OK. That's about it for now. I'll call on them this Sunday. Meanwhile, I have a lot to do before I get started north." Steve got up from the kitchen table, stashed the wad of cash in his windbreaker pocket, and shook hands with Mr. Hess, who nodded, but was unable to utter a word as he followed Steve outside to the sidewalk.

As he pulled away from the curb in his truck, the newly minted bounty hunter flashed a WWII pilot's thumbs-up fist to Gloria's father. Time to head home, make some phone calls, and pack up the surf wagon.

On Saturday morning he called for two kilos of Acapulco Gold fine-cut leaf from Rudy, his *numero uno* source in North Long Beach. Steve only dealt to his surfing crowd—surreptitiously—and only at the beach. He avoided crowded spots for the exchange and always C.O.D. His unbroken rule was absolutely no sales to No-tans, Flatlanders, or Suits. The mostly retail dealing was all the coin Steve needed when combined with his nighttime delivery service. No nine-to-five job as a gofer or clerk. Surfing the AMs year-around when it wasn't windy was his primary focus for the immediate future.

His hand-rolled "newspaper comics" were comprised of less than an ounce each. Steve wore surgical gloves when assembling his packages of mellowness and never touched the paper with his bare hands—no prints. He carried an old wood clothespin to clip onto the goods—no fingers on anything. His "units" always weighed slightly less than an ounce, to keep the ugly prospect of a felony conviction for dealing narcotics, with likely a long prison term, down to a misdemeanor for drug possession, according to the California criminal statute.

Steve's surfboard rack, mounted topside on his trusty but rusty bread wagon panel truck, was fabricated from one-inch copper pipes. The six-foot crossbars were clamped to steel brackets bolted onto the truck's roof. Carpet strips wrapped around the two copper crossbars cushioned a surfboard's smooth belly. The skeg of his Peterson had a hole drilled through it, and a ski-lock cable secured the board to the roof and rack, preventing any surf bum rip-off.

Two-dozen "comic strips" fitted snugly into each copper pipe when packed on his surfboard rack. Screw caps closed the pipe ends tight, safe, and left no detectable smell of grass. Ninety-nine percent safe from discovery by the local blues or narcs.

Through the back door of Alvarado's Mexican Restaurant, just inside the kitchen, Steve picked up his two kilos from Rudy. They'd known each other for some time and pleasantries were not necessary, or even expedient. He peeled off and paid Rudy from his roll of fifties and twenties. The cash and carry "take-out order" was stashed at the bottom of a large grocery sack containing tortillas, tamales, and tacos that were "on the house" according to Rudy. The major element of danger in this risky business transaction was transporting of the goods from the restaurant back to home base. Would the CHP or narcs guess right and look into the bottom of a sack of hot Mexican take-out? Highly unlikely, especially as first they would have to corral his bike.

Getting nailed on the streets by the fuzz while transporting a kilo of Acapulco Gold would leave Lund facing a major felony rap, but once cut and concealed in the surfboard's rack, a drug bust was a low percentage risk he would take.

Safely back home, he pulled Quicksilver into the garage and closed the overhead door, locking it from the inside. After downing two of Rudy's first-rate tacos and a frosty Corona, he slipped on a pair of latex gloves, divided his purchase into equal piles just shy of one-ounce each, and assembled four-dozen "comic-strip" Marys.

After stuffing the surfboard rack pipes and tightly capping the ends, he wrapped the remaining grass in plastic and an old towel. Stashing this package in his locked toolbox, Steve shoved it way back under the garage workbench and helped himself to a second Corona.

He spent Saturday afternoon tracking down Gloria's spacy girlfriends and ex-boyfriends from the list and address book given to him by Mr. Hess. Two of the girlfriends were at Lake Arrowhead for a month and one guy's phone was disconnected. Gloria's closest girlfriends, Darlene and Phyllis, were none too surprised she had split. "Slipped her collar and that short leash for sure," said Darlene. "Maybe she took an impulsive trip to Rosarito Beach down in Baja," Phyllis told him. Highly unlikely she's down in Baja, reasoned Steve. One other friend, Lucille, asked if she could come along with him on his quest. "In your dreams, Lucille, unless you can cook," he told her. Airheads are useless, the bounty hunter decided. Likewise, the ex-boyfriend was of no help—he remarked that Gloria's dad was a hardass German and would do well as a military prison interrogator. So nothing learned from any of them. Tomorrow he would interview Hess's neighbors.

The rest of Saturday faded away with the sunset, with no spell for surfing, as Steve shopped for a week's worth of road food and packed his panel truck with basic camping gear. Several six-packs of Schlitz were added to his "information acquisition kit." More brew could be bought as needed pretty much anywhere along the trip.

The rear section of his '46 Ford panel truck contained a U.S. Navy bunk mattress in a fart sack and one gray wool blanket. A canvas duffle bag held an assortment of beach towels, sweatshirts, and spare shorts. The camp hatchet tucked under the Ford's front seat, a six-inch blade diver's knife, and basic karate provided his security system. Topside was the Steve-made surfboard rack, packed with four-dozen tubes of prime weed and carrying his lashed-down Peterson board.

Unimpressive, ugly, but reliable, the surf wagon was gassed and serviced. The truck's signage touting Paul's Bakery Shop had been partly blotted out with some spray can shots of gray primer. The once-white bakery truck had streams of brown rust stains cascading down its sides from the deteriorating roof gutters. Girlfriends slouched down in the worn out passenger seat when they rode anywhere with him, endeavoring to remain unseen at all costs.

Mechanically, at least, the old Ford bread wagon was fine; he watched the engine's oil and water supply daily since it smoked like an old Kentucky backwoods granny and habitually leaked water. A recent brake job and 'like-new' retreads kept it roadworthy. The butt-ugly surf truck did not resemble what a professional detective would be seen driving around So Cal beaches during his investigation of Gloria's disappearance. The only impression Steve wanted to make, however, was as a surfer prowling around for a certain lost chick—and willing to pay handsomely for information leading to her whereabouts.

Bettie's Answering Service took his late-night package pickup calls for NQA Messenger. Bettie relayed instructions to whatever phone number he'd left with her to call or repeated his messages when he called into her service. "What's up, Bettie Boop?" Steve asked when he dialed in early Saturday evening. Steve told her to expect some important calls from a Mr. Dieter Hess during the next thirty days.

"What kind of mischief are you into now, Buster? Who's this Mr. Hess? Some kind of big time German arms racketeer or drug dealer friend of yours?" Bettie quizzed with a chuckle.

"Don't get bitchy on me, Bettie," replied Steve. "He's the dad of a babe I've been hired to go looking for, so he's OK. He won't call you too often."

"So now you're Dick Tracy or Mr. Bounty Hunter?"

"I'll be searching for her for thirty days, or less, she's a friend, then back to Mr. Numb-nuts on a bike, so don't get your panties twisted in a bunch, BB."

"Watch your mouth, Sonny Boy, or I'll pull the plug on ya, Mr. Smartass!" barked back Bettie.

"OK. OK. Just relax and stay cool. If I pull this job off, there'll be a Franklin with your name on it from me."

"I always enjoy a crisp Ben tucked in my bra, so get on the road and keep me posted," she said.

"Yeah. Also, there's a guy who'll be subbing for me for the next few weeks; name's Bill Bristow. He'll be calling you for NQA pickups. Be nice. I'll be on the bounty hunter job tomorrow with my trusty Dick Tracy wristwatch phone strapped on, and we'll be in touch with you. Gotta go now. *Ciao.*"

Steve rang the doorbell of the first Hess neighbor Sunday morning at ten, and heard door chimes ring inside Mrs. Epstein's residence. The house was a cookie-cutter, Southern California 1920's-style Spanish stucco bungalow with a well-kept lawn. He was about to impatiently punch the doorbell again when the night chain rattled inside and the door creaked slightly open, the night chain still hooked. A wizened, apple-faced, old lady peered out from behind the edge of the door. "What is it, sonny?" the old dame asked.

"I'm a friend of Mr. Hess, your next-door neighbor. His daughter, Gloria, is missing, as you've no doubt heard, and I'm helping out. Could you answer a few questions about the past weekend for me?"

"Yes, all right, as long as you don't come in. I live alone and don't let strangers into my home," the wrinkled crone cautioned.

"Don't worry, no need to come inside, Mrs. Epstein. Did you see or hear Gloria leave home in her station wagon last Sunday night around midnight, and did you notice any strangers in your neighborhood last Sunday?"

"Seems to me the Hess's garage door did open around midnight last Saturday or Sunday night. Can't be sure which night it was. I'm a very light sleeper and awaken easily. Wouldn't know if a car left. I didn't hear one start up. My blinds are closed after dark, and there is a block wall between our houses, as you can see. I didn't see anything unusual hereabouts either. Sorry, I'm not much help to you and Mr. Hess," she apologized.

"That's OK. Thank you for your time. But if you do remember anything else about the weekend, please call Mr. Hess." Steve smiled, turned, and walked back down the walkway.

The mother of the family in the yellow house where Gloria sometimes babysat—a copycat of Mrs. Epstein's bungalow—had nothing to add on her disappearance except to say they would pray for her safe return. So much for the Neighborhood Watch Program on this street, evidently only God was on night duty, thought Steve.

The doorbell of the Brandon residence, a pale-green stucco, pseudo-Spanish-style home, had a note thumbtacked on the doorframe, "PLEASE KNOCK." All the blinds and drapes inside were closed. Steve gave the heavy oak door three sharp knuckle raps and waited. Just as he raised his fist to knock again the door swung wide open. A Rita Hayworth look-a-like redhead in her late thirties stood there smiling, holding a mug of coffee. Her long chestnut hair was shiny wet. Her tanned body was negligently wrapped in a fluffy white robe, loosely bow-tied at her waist.

"What can I do for you, honey?" she asked captivatingly, gazing up and down at the young blond surfer in his shorts and sweatshirt. Voluptuous was the word that popped into Steve's mind as he aped the up and down look she'd given him. The terrycloth swathed her lush figure like frothy meringue. Yum. As she casually leaned against the doorframe, a maroon rosette peeked out from the edge of the robe at him. He wasn't really listening to what she had just said. For a moment, he stood there deaf and dumb as a post.

"Oh, hi! I'm Steve Lund," he finally blurted out. "I'm conducting a missing person inquiry for Mr. Dieter Hess, your next-door neighbor. His daughter, Gloria, has disappeared, and we're trying to locate anyone who may have seen her leave last Sunday night. Maybe you saw her, or someone else, around here that night?"

Roxanne Brandon took a full deep breath, not moving her robe, knowing full well her ample, tanned and freckled breast was being greatly appreciated. "Can't really help you there, Steve. We were gone last weekend to San Diego, and we didn't get home until 1:30 AM Sunday night. Golf. That's my husband's passion. I did hear from Mr. Hess that Gloria is missing. He called and asked me on Monday if we had seen her Sunday night. I told him no. She's a sweet kid. Hope you find her. Want to come in for a cup of coffee or something?" the redhead suggested seductively. "My husband is off golfing, as usual; takes off every Sunday morning with his chums. Doesn't come home until late."

"Love to, Mrs. Brandon, but I can't spare any time right now, even for coffee or something else. Some other Sunday morning—maybe a raincheck? If you do recall anything that may involve Gloria's disappearance, please let Mr. Hess know, will you?"

"Sure, and just call me Roxanne. If you want to do another 'interview,' just stop by any Sunday morning," she said, inhaling deeply and showing off for him.

"Do you know what my favorite flower is, Roxanne?" asked Steve.

"No. Tell me."

"A rose. The Brown Rosette variety."

"Really! I have a couple of those."

"So I noticed, and admired one in full bloom." Steve smiled and casually stroked her exposed brown rosette with his right index finger.

Roxanne didn't move or flinch as they looked evenly into each other's eyes.

"We'll have to start a Brown Rosette Appreciation Society on Sunday mornings, just for the two of us," whispered Steve.

"Yes. Let's do that. I'm looking forward to some appreciation too."

"Wish I had time right now, but I just don't."

"The rose garden will be open most Sunday mornings for you, Steve. Free admission, so stop by for a showing."

"I'll plan on doing just that, Roxanne, and soon. See you later, and I mean literally," he said, turning away slowly and strolling back to his truck, still greatly aroused in the trunks. He got in and threw a kiss to her as she stood leaning against the doorway, watching him.

How about those speckled Irish beauties? I'll have to stop by on Golf Sunday, just as soon as I'm done with this search business, he mused, and headed to Huntington to cool his passions in the surf. Last chance to catch some gnarly rights before heading up the coast on Monday.

Swells at the Bluffs were rolling in like a wave machine at three and four feet with the incoming tide, and thankfully the afternoon chop had not kicked in yet. He surfed hard and fast for over two hours, riding everything that jacked up, big and little. On the last head-high wave, he stroked hard into a closing peeler right, dropped down, and quickly shot straight right across the inside, outrunning the curl folding right behind the Peterson's tail. Sometimes surfing is as good as sex, and it lasts longer, he thought to himself.

Time to head home and finish packing up. I'll check again with Uncle Bert and fill him in on what I've done so far, the tired and salty boarder thought. Might not mention my Roxanne "interview."

Monday brought a warm, low-overcast summer morning. A windshield-obscuring wet fog was shifting and drifting about at street level. No success in reaching Gloria's shrink at nine-fifteen AM. "She's attending a conference in San Francisco until Wednesday," the soft-spoken secretary stated primly. Dr. Grayson's brain would have to be picked later.

The surfer-detective sported his usual Sherlock Holmes in California traveling gear: a sleeveless gray sweatshirt, cut-off Levis, and Mexican huaraches. A battered Timex wristwatch hung from the rearview mirror by a seawater-worn canvas strap. "This shitty weather is not helping," Steve grumbled as he traveled cautiously along the Highway One seacoast below Pacific Palisades. The panel truck's headlights were on and the single wiper slapped away futilely at the mist-clouded windshield.

Steve and Mr. Hess had discussed his plan to start by canvassing the northernmost surfing beaches and then backtrack to the Santa Monica Bay section. Next, he'd briefly reconnoiter the Manhattan to Redondo strands. The final beaches to cover would be the remaining hundred-mile stretch from Seal Beach to Ocean Beach in San Diego. It was a wide net to cast for one small mermaid.

Funky Venice and Santa Monica, even with their weirdos and musclemen in Speedos, might be promising beach towns to find the missing eighteen-year-old runaway, and they'd have to be checked out, along with the rest of the So Cal coastline.

High-style Malibu living was way too upscale for the average John and Jane. Rich bitches and pseudo-starlets with opulent Hollywood sugar daddies were the predominant denizens of the Malibu enclave ensconced in the seaside playground sandbox.

Farther up the coastline at surfing spots in Ventura and Santa Barbara counties, loners in old pickup campers, or decayed panels, and the ever-present juvie locals prevailed. It would be an uncrowded weekday scene up that way at the surf breaks, but worth spending a few days to search, catch some waves, and pass out fliers of Gloria among the hardcore surfers' ratty old delivery panels and weathered woodies.

Cruising on up the Coast Highway One, Steve pulled over at the construction site of a monster home north of Malibu to scrounge some scrap wood for his beach campfires. Green Douglas Fir two-by-fours are so full of sap that the chunks frequently explode, as if plugged with black gunpowder, when a scrap wood fire is blazing on the beach. Every few minutes a two-by would go off, showering fiery sparks onto bare skin and clothes. He'd have to make sure his heavily waxed board wasn't lying close to the fire; otherwise it could easily become a ten-foot flaming matchstick.

Back on the road, Steve cranked his driver's-side window down to inhale deeply from the wet ocean fog drifting across the slick onyx highway, pungent with a seaweed-iodine sea salt tang that cleanses the brain. He left the window down until the chill and wetness got to be a little too cool for comfort.

"I wonder where that Gloria ran off to," he grumbled to himself. "She's cutting into my surfing days."

The blue-gray ocean was flatter than Mono Lake. The beaches of Malibu, Point Dume, and Zuma were fogged in solid. Nobody out.

With the layer of morning ocean fog flat and thick below, the hillside mansions speckled along the coastline resembled isolated Pacific island atolls. Gloria could easily find a live-in maid or nanny situation in one of those mega houses, mused Steve, but if so, he knew that he'd have a hard time finding out.

Crossing the L.A.-Ventura County line, where Highway 23 dead-ends at the Pacific Ocean, Steve stopped at the gloomy beach to chat with a pair of high school surfers from Moorpark. Better to be sitting on a fogged-in beach with no surf than sweltering in Simi Valley, they told him. Said they would keep a sharp eye out for Gloria and the Velzy.

Usually, County Line was a primo surfing break. Not today. Nobody about and nobody out. The Pacific remained as still as a flat cat spread-eagled on the roadway. I'll paper this stretch with fliers on the way back from Santa Barbara, thought Steve.

Sea mist and salty spume coated the panel truck's windshield with a layer of grimy film that the Ford's single wiper lashed at ineffectively. By eleven the sun had burned the obscuring shoreline grayness back to the fringes of Highway 1 where the wall of stubborn fog stayed put over the sea as if it were being held behind an invisible dam.

Beyond Solimar, the highway became a rough, sinuous two-lane stretch that was bulldozed and blacktopped between the rugged, earthquake-prone mountainside and the jagged ocean shoreline. Point Mugu was desolate, as usual, with parched, chaparral-covered mountains on the right and the rocky beach zone on the left. The pockmarked road, cutting an asphalt track between mountain and beach was littered as always with fist-sized jagged rocks and scattered scree.

Good pit stops beyond Point Mugu would be Oxnard and then Ventura, he reminded himself, as he instinctively yanked the surf wagon hard left, barely missing a softball-sized rock in the right lane. What the hell is a Mugu, he wondered. Probably a garbled American Indian name for Ugly Place, like a lot of other misnamed Southwest landmarks.

Trying to track down the yellow Velzy and its owner somewhere within five coastal counties was going to be like hunting for a specific chunk of driftwood on an isolated beach, or a teen-age virgin in Tijuana. Steve ruminated on this and other thoughts, such as where he might find the best breaks, as he drove on to Oxnard through miles of bean fields.

Sometime after noon he stopped at the south edge of town for a burger basket and frosted mug of root beer at the

A&W Drive-in. Oxnard resembled a farm town transplanted from the Midwest to Ventura County, California. Young hayseed studs, parked side-by-side in their dusty Chevy pickups at the A&W, would have fit right into the milieu of Emporia, Kansas.

Six local yokels in the drive-in lot were all wearing misshapen, straw cowboy hats and faded blue denim shirts with the sleeves hacked off—Paul Newman style. Tri-colored, blue-eyed, cattle dogs sat in the bed of each pickup truck. Odds-on these aggies never frequent their local surfing beaches, except to run their dogs around and drink beer, mused the outsider. Surfers were of a different cut, seldom away from their beaches, and rarely seen in Oxnard.

Oxnard wasn't much known for its surfing spots, but Steve did drive by to eyeball Mandalay and McGrath Beaches. Flat and empty. Two Seabees from Port Hueneme were trying half-heartedly to paddle on ratty surfboards into some two-foot shoreline mush, with little success. When they came out of the water, he gave them a flier, but it was doubtlessly a waste of paper.

It was mid-afternoon by the time he checked into a stop-and-flop motel, his best-of-the-worst choice in the time-warped Thirties-era of downtown Ventura. Steve planned to track down his local surfer contact at the beach bar under the Municipal Pier. He also called Mr. Hess, who had no news except to say Gloria had cashed out her bank account during the week before she skipped. Another fact that made it highly likely her Sunday night exit was planned in advance.

The thirsty detective drove the two miles from his stop-and-flop to Ventura's warm and hazy main beach strand at four-thirty and parked adjacent to the old wooden munici-pal pier. A good day for a flatlander family to quickly obtain the red lobster look. Ultra-violet rays penetrate through the overcast and haze, just like on a bright sunny day, frying unsuspecting beachgoers to a crisp.

Kenny Estep from Newport Beach had told Steve to contact "Mitchell" at the beer bar tucked under the city pier. Kenny E. was Steve's longtime surfing buddy from Orange County and another Huntington habitué.

Though concealed under the creosote-tarred pier pil-ings, the local's-only bar was still fairly-crowded, serving pints of Olympia draft in mugs freezer-cold enough to "frost your balls" according to Kenny E. "Gimme a tap Oly and a couple of your pickled eggs, will ya, barkeep?" or-dered Steve as he sauntered past the taps toward the rear of the musty beer bar. The barely twenty-one, sun-bleached barman, clad in a faded sleeveless blue-and-yellow UCLA sweatshirt and khaki denim shorts, pulled a draught of cold brew and settled the icy mug and a pair of purple eggs in front of the neophyte detective. Steve had tented two dollar bills plus a crisp Lincoln on the bar top. Taking a long pull on the icy draft, he said to the Bruin fan, "Keep the bills, mate. Seen Mitchell around?"

The heavyset blond barkeep smiled at the generous tip. "Not yet, friend. He'll probably show around five or six."

"Point me out to him when he shows, will ya? I'm a friend of a friend, not the Fuzz," added Steve as he settled in to wait on the padded barstool, savoring his first, frosty brew and munching on one of the spicy eggs. The barman gave a noncommittal nod and headed back down the bar to his taps and mugs.

Nearing five-thirty, Steve was deep into his second Oly and had polished off a second pair of lavender hen fruit when a stocky and weathered, sandy-headed guy in a faded green tank top and yellow cutoffs sauntered into the dim and noisy bar and ordered a draft. The barman directed a few low words at the tank-topped surfer, nodding towards the newcomer sitting at the rear of the bar.

"Hey, ol' Joey said you were looking for me," the burly blond said, offering a firm handshake while easing onto the barstool next to Steve.

"If you're Mitchell, yeah, I am. Name's Steve Lund; I'm a surfing bud of Kenny Estep's. I'm up this way to check out some surf spots, among other things. Estep said to look you up and say Hi, and that maybe you could give me the skinny on some Ventura and Santa Barbara breaks. They wouldn't have to be your private spots," joked Steve.

"Can do for an old friend of Estep's, 'specially for a dude who's buyin' the brews. Spent last summer with the 'Step on Santa Monica Bay, surfing from Malibu to Redondo. Man, Venice has some pretty strange squirrels and plenty of kinky babes wandering around on the boardwalk. A real Barnum and Bailey. Rent's cheap, though. And the water's a good ten degrees warmer there than here. Had a blast!"

The visiting sleuth pulled a flier on Gloria from his pocket, unfolded it, and laid it face up on the bar. "By the way, Mitchell, here's the other thing I'm up this way to see about. Think you might've seen this babe or board up this way? She's just a bunny, so she could be around here trying out the two- and three-footers beside the pier."

The chunky surfer held the sheet between his stubby thumb and index finger, rotating it so the sunlight from outside would show the details of Gloria's photo. "What kind of stick is she holding? Looks like a Venice Velzy."

"Yeah, good guess. A mustard yellow one, about eight-two."

"Haven't seen that board or the broad around here. Think I'd remember her, nice. What's the deal on this babe? Stole your stick, then jilted you and split?" Mitchell quizzed Steve with a wicked smile.

"Nah. Just that she's missing. Been over a week since she's been seen at her stomping grounds around Long Beach and Huntington. Family and friends are worried and would like her to call home, that's all. The second phone number on the sheet is her father's. I'm just doin' him a favor, lookin' around for her. My phone service is the top one. If you see or hear anything about her, just call, collect. Incidentally, there's a grand in it for you. Guaranteed."

"So then, you're a bounty hunter. I get it now—the surf-er searcher. O.K., you're on. Is this babe alone?"

"Alone and with wheels. Details are all in the flier there. Her ride is a pea-green '48 Chevy wagon. This is a legit, off-the-top deal. C.O.D.," assured Steve. "Lemme buy you a fresh brew. We'll check out the sunset from the boardwalk while you fill me in on a few good surf breaks up the coast. I've been in this cave long enough."

"Deal," the local agreed. They picked up a pair of fresh, cold Olys; Steve paid the tab with another fiver, leaving the change for Joey. The two surfers strolled out onto the warm hazy strand and sat on the low cement beach wall.

"Well, Steve, for starters, drive north to Pitas Point, Seacliffs, and Two County Line just up the coast, 'bout five to ten miles. I'll show you on the map in my van. There are usually decent swells breaking at Pitas on the incoming tide, even in summer.

"Carpenteria, landmark's the giant Santa Claus, might be good if a north swell develops. Farther north, beyond Santa Barb, are El Capitan and Refugio. Those are up a few miles past Goleta. Usually, nice glassy morning breaks 'll come in when you're south side of Refugio's river mouth sand bar. The bar may have washed out by now from the ocean current. Haven't been up that way for a few weeks. That's about it for the main surf breaks up this way, ol' buddy. I ain't tellin' anyone about my private ones, friend of Estep's or no. You don't need to know. Refugio is far enough north. You'd freeze your *cajones* off surfing any-where beyond Pt. Conception," counseled the local water-man as he drained the last of his mug.

They had another "last round" on Steve while watching the obscured orange orb slide over the indistinct watery horizon. When they walked to Mitchell's van, Steve handed over a few more Gloria fliers to pass around and Mitchell pointed out on the map where the popular surf breaks were located. The two said "See you later" and Steve drove off—sloshing in suds.

Mucho brews and four purple eggs were enough to keep hunger pangs away until morning. Steve steered the panel truck cautiously back to his fleabag motel room and zonked out.

Tuesday morning, 9 a.m. The groggy private eye checked out of the motel, head throbbing, and had his coffee fix with two hot cinnamon rolls, joining the geezer crowd at the Downtown Coffee Shop on Thompson Street. Finally feeling halfway human, after downing two aspirins on top of the coffee, he started up the bread wagon, checked the water and oil, and pulled onto Highway 1, headed north. The not quite head-high sets were rolling in at one hundred yards out at Pitas Point. A half-dozen surfers were out, jockeying for position in the lineup. No sign of the pea-green Chevy, the missing Gloria, or the Velzy.

Steve couldn't resist the temptation as the consistent washboard sets rolling into shore beckoned, so he spent an hour or so working the Point's four and five footers until he hauled himself out of the surf feeling guilty. He gave out fliers to four boarders on the beach who were waxing up and left another one with two friendly Asian teens, Freddy and Sammy, who were just unloading their boards.

He stopped briefly at the Carpenteria/Santa Claus section, but an onshore breeze was already starting to kick up small whitecaps, making conditions there choppy and sloppy. Two bronzed surfers from Ojai were sacked out on the warm sandy beach. Steve handed them a flier and gave his "missing girl" spiel. Time to call it a short day and hit the next stop, Santa Barbara, for the night.

The bottom end of State Street, Santa Barbara's main drag, was mere blocks from Stearns Wharf. Touristy State Street offered a selection of skanky motels near the Southern Pacific train tracks that ran the daily Daylight and Starlight up and down the scenic Pacific Coast. The novice private eye decided to check into the "better of the worst." State Street Motel was a nondescript, lime green, one-story concrete block with a blinking, neon "vacancy" sign. The bunker had a dozen or so cubicles, each with a single, barred window and a blank steel door brush-painted white and developing rust cankers.

"Six dollars, no checks, cash in advance" the old Indian—from India—said.

"I'll bet your last name is Patel," said Steve, as he handed over six singles.

"Yes, sir, that is correct," replied the Indian, not smiling as he handed over a brass room key stamped Room #2. Steve knew that most of the budget motels in California were owned and operated by Patels. Family run with no hired help to rip them off—and no one to pay even minimum wages.

Might as well be housed in the Ventura County slammer on a DUI for free instead of cooped up in this cell-by-the-sea, wasting six bucks, thought the sandy traveler.

What the hell, it's only for another solo stop-and-flop night on this so-far-fruitless outing.

Steve dropped a dime to dial his Santa Barbara surfer contact, Zack, from the motel's pay phone. "Zack's off on a surfari, North Shore of Oahu, man, and won't be back for three weeks," his roomie stated. He got the street address anyway so he could drop off a few fliers to the roomie. Wouldn't hurt to spread the word around the Santa Barb area beaches.

Lund phoned Mr. Hess at five-thirty to check in and find out if anything had developed at his end. The LBPD was stuck on empty, still treating Gloria's vanishing act as a runaway—which indubitably it was. No promising leads from the want ads in the beach cities' newspapers' classified sections, nor from her friends or the fliers. "I'll call you again in a few days then. Hang in there," Steve told Hess. He seems to be taking his daughter's disappearance pretty well now, and isn't so freaked out, the young investigator thought as he hung up the phone.

Unwashed and salty, still in swim trunks and zoris, the surfer strolled past trinket- and T-shirt-filled tourist shops along the long, wooden Stearns Wharf. At the weather-beaten walk-up seafood stand located at the pier's far end, he ravenously consumed a basket of fish and chips and drained two longneck Lucky Lagers. Finishing off the fries, with the unwanted help of a seagull buddy, he slowly sauntered back, savoring the casual California atmosphere of the seaside town. Another longneck, a long hot shower, and flopping early into the lumpy sack would eliminate having to stare at four dingy-white blank walls and the barred window. The picture on the small black-and-white

TV flickered and fluttered like a silent movie snowstorm as the private eye's lids closed for the day.

Next morning the sleep-saturated searcher got an early eight-thirty kick-start with a syrup-laden short stack washed down with three cups of coffee at the Wharf Café. He gassed up and serviced his rusty Ford at the State Street Shell and pointed its nose again up Highway 1. The weather was gloomy and everything wet, typical for June and July on the California coast.

It was already 9:45 when he rolled into the nearly deserted parking lot of El Capitan Beach, a few miles north of Goleta, just as the morning fog was clearing up. Mitchell had told him that El Cap was a flat sandy beach at a small stream's mouth, and the resulting sandbar creates an ocean hump that more often than not offers a nice ride.

Two ratty Ford woodies and a beater Plymouth panel truck with two boards lashed on top were parked near the beach, but there were no other signs of life. Wonder if everyone's got the Tuesday morning blearies, or is in the sack hosting chicks, the visitor asked himself.

An unbroken chain of rights breaking shoulder high about ninety yards out in the murky morning light looked enticing. "Might as well catch a few of those nice righties going off while the woodie boys are sleeping it off," thought Steve, parking the Ford a short distance away.

He got out, unloaded his board, and strapped a sheath containing an anodized diver's knife with a serrated six-inch blade onto his right leg. He picked up his board and trotted down to shore and into the ocean.

Straddling his log just outside the surf line, taking a short breather, he spotted human life forms in slow motion on the beach approaching the trio of parked cars. Surfers or Neanderthals? I'll soon find out. He took a few deep strokes and caught the next wave to shore, hopping off his Peterson right at the sand. A nifty move, more for show than anything. Strolling up to the four shaggy local bucks slugging down a morning brewski breakfast while waxing up their boards, he spoke up casually. "Hey guys, I'm Steve, from Long Beach, just trying out your first-rate break up here. Mitchell, in Ventura, said it was probably OK to hang a few at this spot, just as long as I stayed off your waves. Usual territorial rules apply, locals first. Cool with you?"

The two gnarly older boarders both nodded once. The two others were oblivious, still out of it, waxing their sticks and sipping brew, as if Steve didn't exist.

"Whatcha packin' that shark sticker for when you're surfin' up here?" asked the sly-looking, dark-haired older guy.

"Case I get snagged in the kelp, or meet up with the man in the gray flannel suit out there," replied Steve. "Its blade is razor sharp."

"Kin I see your shark sticker for a minnit?" said the sly one.

"Sorry, 'fraid not," said Steve. "An old Samurai creed I practice. Comes out of the sheath, the blade must taste blood. I'd have to nick myself or stick it into something else to draw blood. That's my rule, so guess it stays put for now."

"Sounds kinda weird to me, Steve from Long Beach. You part Jap or sumpthin'?" said the dark-haired one.

"Nah. Do I look like a Celestial, or somethin? Heard it in a movie, and the rule just sounded kinda cool to me, so now that's my rule. You guys surf this section of the coast all the time, right? Listen, I'm looking for a missing surfer girl from Long Beach. Be willing to give you a few samples of primo leaf for any info you might have."

"What's your angle here, Jack? Sellin' dope?" replied the older Alfa surfer, green eyes glaring. This guy had shoulder-length, bleached-out peroxided hair, a sharp, crooked nose, and looked to be about twenty-eight. Probably at least six-foot-two and weighing two-twenty plus, including his puffed-out belly and a muffin-top roll lapping over ragged khaki shorts. Not the type you want to mess with all alone at a desolate beach site, thought Steve.

"No, man, not into selling pot, or meth either. I just want to show you a flier on the missing girl. Be right back with it... and a little leaf, just as an incentive," promised Steve as he turned and trotted to his truck. He pulled out six Gloria fliers from the front seat and surreptitiously took two tubes of leaf from his surf rack, then relocked the Ford. Steve handed the fliers and grass to Big Alfa man, who seemed to be the main *honcho*.

"Any of you seen this girl or her yellow surfboard around your beaches? She's missing, and so is her green Chevy wagon. There's a nice bundle of cash, a grand, in it for anyone who helps locate her. Keep those fliers handy because the information on her and the contact phone numbers are on the sheet."

Alfa Dude passed out the fliers to the others, but kept the grass to himself, stashing it in his shorts. None of the others changed their facial expression or raised a voice in protest.

"Haven't seen your missing babe, Jack. But thanks for the weed. Got any more you want to unload?" the big Viking finally replied after reading over the flier.

"Nah, sorry man, I'm not a dealer or a narc, and I don't have any spare grass. Just a pinch or two to help spur memories of the missin' lass," said Steve, eyeing Alpha warily.

"Don't think there's room for you out there any longer, Long Beach Stevo. This ain't Mitchell's territory either. Better move on out."

"OK, guys. I'm just a surfer looking for a girl. If you do spot her, just drop a dime, and a grand, cash, will come your way. I'm headed back south now," replied Steve as calmly as he could.

The waterman departed quickly, giving the surly quartet of pirates a quick backhand wave as he toted his board back to the truck, but got no response. Damn glad I didn't get worked over and mugged right there, thought the inexperienced sleuth. Not a smart move on my part with four-to-one odds, even with my six-inch shark slicer.

No point in searching farther north. Point Conception is 34 degrees latitude and that's where Southern California ends. The Pacific Ocean gets rough and chilly beyond there, not a likely place for a So Cal babe unless she's heading all the way up to SF, or beyond. Time to backtrack south on the so-far-*nada-mucho* quest for Miss Gloria Hess.

The searcher headed down the coast along the sparsely populated Goleta coastline, stopping briefly to check out Refugio Beach. No surfers out or about, probably on account of the dinky waves. A covey of flatlander campers lounged in the shade of a stand of giant eucalyptus trees. He'd canvass every surfing spot and the beach city communities from Santa Barbara to the LA County line, passing out fliers and stopping in at the local police stations along the way back south to leave the fuzz a few too. A long day of bird-dogging for Gloria.

It was getting dark when he stopped alongside Highway 1, just north of the Ventura/Los Angeles County line near Point Mugu, a windy and chilly off-road spot on a desolate and rocky beach. His scrap wood fire was soon blazing hot, popping with minor explosions and fireworks.

He jacked open a can of Dennison's chili, tore off the label, and set the can next to the beach fire to heat up, then cracked open a brew. When the chili was bubbling hot, he retrieved it with a pair of pliers he kept in the truck, and set it down on the beach. Slicing off a large chunk of San Francisco sourdough with his diver's knife, he settled in to devour his cowboy dinner of chili, bread, and beer. After cleaning off the spoon and knife at the water's edge, he took a piss into the campfire and crawled into the cold bread truck for the night.

Steve called Mr. Hess the next morning from the pay phone at the nearby Sycamore Grove campground. No news, good or bad. He assured Mr. Hess it was still way early in the hunt and he was keeping to his Plan A.

LA County line was still pretty empty shortly before ten. Steve downed a cold Sara Lee snail and a pint of acidic, black coffee from a roadside gas station's mini-mart and hit the beach boys there with a fistful of fliers. He gabbed a bit with a covey of teen surfers; two of them from Camarillo claimed they'd seen a green Chevy wagon parked there a few days ago with a surfboard inside it. They hadn't noticed any girl, but one remembered seeing a stuffed dog on the front seat.

The wagon, surfboard, and dog combo was the first concrete lead—or at least the first possible clue—the searcher had come up with so far. But it had been a few days back, and the teens weren't even quite sure precisely what day it had been, so Steve decided it wasn't worth staying in the area. The Camarillo duo and their buddies promised to call in if the same pea-green wagon reappeared in their territory. Trolling with a thousand-dollar bill seemed to attract everyone's attention, just as Uncle Bert had predicted.

Zuma was a trudge: two miles long, wide, flat, and all deep sand. Surfers were scattered in small buddy bunches. Mostly guys with tagalong babes hung out on the westward beach until the afternoon wind kicked up and knocked the waves down. Teens communed between the lifeguard main towers. It took Steve a couple of hours to paper the parked vehicles and chat briefly with the surfers lolling on the warm beach. Nobody had seen or heard about Princess Gloria but they were interested in the reward. He knew most of them would drop a dime on her for the grand offered if she showed up.

Still backtracking south along the rugged shoreline, Steve made his next stop to see two of his knob-kneed surfing cronies, Leo and Larry, who'd recently turned horse caretakers. They were working at Malibu Stables, adjacent to the exclusive Malibu Equestrian Center and directly across Highway 1 from one of the premier surfing spots of Southern California.

According to Leo, they were furnished with bunkhouse quarters, plus there were other "incentives" for the young stud wranglers. Early each weekday morning the two horse tenders would throw some grain for their sleek steeds, head for the glassy breaks across the highway, surf 'til nine, then back to mucking out horse stalls 'til noon. They had Sundays off to rip non-stop from dawn 'til dusk. Not a lifetime profession for them, but it sure beat working for The Man at Safeway, stacking shelves and bagging groceries inside all day for minimum coin.

When Steve found them that afternoon, the two were ripping and cutting at Malibu Point, a short way up the road from the stables. They invited him to stick around to surf with them and sack out overnight at their bunkhouse digs.

"Deal," said Steve without hesitation. Malibu Point's break was jacking up some fine four-foot peaks and long right shoulders. A workday for most people, only a handful of locals were out in the offshore lineup.

"Just take your turn and don't cut off the locals," cautioned Leo as he paddled back out with Steve. Leo was twenty, short and slim. His reddish-brown crew cut was prickly as Dakota wheat stubble, just like his attitude. The jockey-sized wrangler stroked hard into a closing peeler right, dropped down into the center of the bowl, and cut a zigzag pattern up and down the wave face, outrunning the curl folding fast behind him. Very cool moves and a tough act to follow.

Larry was a different breed than Leo, with an ordered and easy style about him. An ordinary looking surfer, standard issue Italian, standing an inch under six feet, with black curly hair that fell to his shoulders and nearly onto his Tuscan nose. His mind was quirky—some thought that "weird" was a more apt definition. One of his favorite pranks was to saunter through a parking lot and wang bang his flat hand on the side panel of a car that was just backing out. He would then yell and start hopping around on one foot like a run-over dog, freaking out the rattled female driver—usually a young female. Then Larry would stop and bow deeply to her, smile and walk away. In the ocean he made surfing look as if anybody could just paddle out and catch his first wave ever with no sweat. "Never miss, No Sweat Larry."

A few minutes before five, the trio strapped their boards onto the roof rack of Steve's Ford and drove back to Malibu Stables. "Back to our hay and grain grinders," said Larry.

"Say, Lorenzo, heard from your old flame, Gloria, recently? I've been hired by her father to find her. She split."

"I was wondering what you were doing so far away from home on a weekday. So she cut out on the old bastard, did she? I'm not too surprised. Her dad's an asshole, if you ask me. Why should I tell you if we've seen her around up here?" groused Larry.

"Because I'm your old surfing buddy and pot supplier, that's why. Also, there's a grand in your hand if you rat her out. Since you have no intention of marrying her, you might as well have the reward instead of some other pothead. What do you say?" implored the detective.

"Yeah, OK. Gloria was up here this week. Sunday, it was. Just passing through, she said. Didn't say if she was headed north or south. Had her new board in the wagon. I tried to talk her into staying overnight to party, but no dice, damn it. Said she had to be somewhere on Monday. Maybe she'll be back. If she shows up again, I'll be sure to keep her in sight until you show up with the cash. A grand, huh? You're right, ol' buddy. I'm the lecherous kind, not the marrying kind."

Back at the ranch it was time for the two buckaroos to get with their chores, shoveling horseshit, brushing down their nippy charges. "Did you know these pricy thoroughbreds have the equivalent mentality of that bucktoothed gopher over there near the fence pushing up that mound of dirt?" asked Leo.

"You may have that right, but you don't get paid to groom and feed bucktoothed rodents, do you?" laughed Steve.

"No. You're right. We feed, brush, and exercise these fancy steeds so rich old farts and their hooker mistresses, trophy wives, and comely teen daughters can come out here afternoons and weekends to trot them around on the trails and get their jollies off," remarked Leo.

"We're not bitching though. Shoveling horse plops is a great workout for the biceps and shoulders. Also, we get our fair share of 'bunkhouse drop-ins,' after hours," smiled Larry the Letcher, pointing out the hand painted sign posted over the bunkhouse door "Fillies Broken In Here."

"We should have a couple of fillies, Michelle and Suzanne, coming by about nine or ten tonight for a little dancing and prancing. I'll phone and see if they can rustle up an ugly old mare for you to ride. Otherwise, you'll be forced to just take a long hot shower by yourself," ragged Leo.

"Fine with me. As long as she doesn't look or smell *too* horsey or step on my toes with her hoofs."

"These fillies are high spirited and definitely not barn smelly, as you might be lucky enough to discover for yourself," assured Larry.

Just after nine-thirty a brand new, pearl white Chrysler Town and Country station wagon cruised into the stable's yard and three leggy horse ladies alighted. The two ponytail blonds and the flapper-cut brunette looked to be somewhere in their mid-thirties, well groomed, highly maintained, and self-assured. Trophy wives out after dark, kicking up their heels. The trio wore tan, whipcord riding breeches, Western shirts that were partially unbuttoned, and highly polished cordovan leather riding boots. The horse-loving trio looked frisky and ready to party.

"Welcome, ladies, to the Malibu tavern and dancehall. We've got plenty of margie mix and ice. What brand of cactus juice did you bring to the party?" asked Leo.

"A full liter of Hornitos Reposado straight from Ensenada, very potent stuff," replied Suzanne, the big blond with the augmented mammary glands.

"Oh, my God! That means we'll have to finish off the whole liter tonight. It won't go to waste on us thirsty cowhands. You certainly have excellent taste in tequila, as well as men," said Larry.

"It won't go to waste if we three have anything to do with it—so don't melt down on us," said Michelle.

"Never worry," replied Steve. "Us mustangs are not about to melt or disappoint tonight!"

"There's two bottles of cab left over from last week's shindig if anyone is interested. Ritas are quicker but it's your choice," said Leo.

"Ritas around," everyone yelled.

"Stranger Steve, this raven-haired flapper filly is Delores. Treat her nice—no whip," remarked Leo as the sextet trooped into the dance hall-bunkhouse.

"Hi, Steve. Think I'll stick to margies and Marlboros instead of the usual brews and grass," grinned green-eyed Delores. "How about fixing me a margie on the rocks, no salt, to kick this party off?" she said while lightly stroking his arm with her green enameled fingernails.

"Whatever turns you on, and produces the desired chemistry," smiled Steve as he patted her ass and headed for the kitchen. "Tequila Sunrise Special—no salt—coming up!"

Leo lit some candles around the bunkhouse and turned off the bunkhouse lights while Larry placed a stack of LPs on the record player for the evening's dancing and prancing. Smooth dance platters of Lionel Hampton, Count Basie, Cab Calloway, Duke Ellington, and Dizzy Gillespie, intermixed with Bill Haley and B.B. King for spice, plus Hank Williams for Country Western flavor. "These discs oughta' set the mood until the candlelight and booze activates the primal heat," grinned Larry, the DJ. Not a lot of conversation took place over the next hour or so. Just lots of dancin' and prancin' and drinkin'.

"Michelle and I are going out to the barn and listen to the owls hoot. Don't come looking for us until midnight, ya' hear? These fillies have to skedaddle home to daddy by twelve or it will bring heaps of grief to all. Just come banging on the old barn door and we'll knock off the hooting," laughed Larry as the couple swayed unsteadily out the bunkhouse door.

A few minutes later Leo announced, "Enough of this horseplay—time for some riding lessons. Lights out! Women on top in the saddle—we're just along for the ride, Steve," he whispered as he blew out the candles, leaving the record player on with some Ellington mood music playing.

The two couples split to opposite ends of the dark bunkhouse, racing to find out how quickly tight boots and riding breeches could be pried off in the pitch black room. Bill Haley and the Comets were just getting into the merits of "Rock the Joint" when the mattresses began to bounce and the bunk beds were squeaking away.

"Damn it, Delores! You're gonna crack my ribs with that scissors grip! Relax," gasped Steve into her ear.

"Sorry. I was thinking I was riding a bucking bronc in a rodeo and didn't want to get thrown," she breathed raggedly.

"You're not about to get tossed, considering the grip your legs have on me, so just loosen up a bit and enjoy the ride, OK?"

"Yeah, oh yeah! Oooh yeah!" she yelled out.

The brilliant morning sun shone through the bunkhouse window way too early and lit up Steve's face. A Brazilian drummer pounded away inside his throbbing skull. Two Anacins and a large cup of instant coffee made a deeper acid pit in his belly, so he downed two bananas to quiet the turmoil inside.

The other two bronc busters were still lying motionless, zonked out and lonesome in their bunks. He left them a dozen Gloria fliers to spread around the Malibu beaches and six "comic strip" packets of leaf for their next "night ride." The visiting boarder reminisced that the surfing and party time had been most memorable. It would be well worth repeating later in the summer.

The Malibu stallions did know how to pick a filly and party! A scrap of paper with a phone number and "D" scribbled on it had been left on his pillow. He tiptoed out, cranked up the surf wagon, watered it, and headed south.

At the Malibu Beach Market, he squeezed his rusty and ratty panel truck in between a cream-yellow Mercedes-Benz convertible and a racing green Jag XK coupe. Strolling into the market, a blondie clad only in a bright yellow bikini sashayed out. She slid into the ragtop Benz without a glance his way—ignoring Steve's stare. Another guy's wheels and his trophy would be the guess, unless her parents were flush.

He bought two oversize hoagies for lunch and dinner and a couple of Schlitz six-packs to restock the truck. A quart of milk and a large, glazed snail returned his growling gut to only a mild churning sensation. Steve's ribs still hurt, but it was worth it.

Time to check in this morning with Gloria's father and then hit the last eight surfing beaches before reaching Santa Monica. There was nothing new from Mr. Hess. Steve reminded him that the most likely area that Gloria may be in was yet to be canvassed and filled him in on the possible "Gloria sighting"—maybe her car too—up near the Ventura

County Line. He could hear Hess catch his breath over the phone at the news. He didn't mention that she'd been in Malibu last Sunday to see Larry; too much to explain and for what? He climbed back into his rusty, dusty bread truck and headed farther south.

It took Steve the morning and all afternoon to cover the eight surfing spots below Malibu Point: Carbon Canyon, La Costa, Las Flores, Big Rock, Las Tunas, Topanga, Sunset, and Pacific Palisades. Las Tunas and Topanga were the most crowded and had the best surfing. Amphibious surfers were on the sand or floating on their surfboards just outside the lineup, waiting their turn. A polite bunch of locals—rare. Steve pasted Gloria fliers onto the windshield of any likely surfer's vehicle, and touted about the full grand of reward money to the local boarders on the beaches, but there was no word of her whereabouts nor any reported sightings.

The no-luck searcher pulled wearily into the Will Rogers State Beach parking area, north side of Santa Monica proper, just before sunset. A foreboding fogbank was lurking in the bay about a mile offshore. The orange globe in the west flattened out and melted into the hazy grayness where it was quickly extinguished.

Steve took a running dive into the surf and swam hard for a few minutes, then relaxed on the still warm sand and munched down his remaining hoagie, flushing dinner down with two tepid cans of Schlitz. Might as well crash here for the night, he thought. The local *gendarmerie* is not likely to roust me in my truck if a thick fog settles in here tonight, obscuring the parking lot from the highway. Sacking out overnight in your vehicle within the city limits of Santa Monica is definitely not a smart thing to do. He heard the SaMo cops would recite the "No Overnighters" municipal code violation to sleepy you at three AM while calling for SM Tow on their police radio. The midnight fuzz reportedly received a share of the tow bill, according to a friend of Steve's who had gone to SaMo High.

Next morning the dripping-wet panel truck rolled out of the foggy and still-empty state beach lot. No cops around or citation on the windshield this time. He kicked off his day by stopping at a roadside market at Chautauqua and Coast Highway for a large scalding mug of coffee and a raisin snail. Canvassing Santa Monica's extensive beach area was next on the "To Do" list after first ministering to the needs of the old Ford.

The three-story, white stone building, situated smack downtown on Main Street and a block from the Pacific Ocean, housed Santa Monica's City Hall and Police Department. Steve parked across the busy four-lane boulevard, grabbed a few fliers and jaywalked across to the monolithic structure's main entrance. An overstuffed sergeant in shiny blue serge, deeply engrossed in his *Police Gazette* magazine, manned the Police Department desk on the right, just inside the door.

"Howdy, Sarge. Would you please see that your beach patrol division gets these missing person fliers? The vital information is typed on the back. She is a friend of mine and she's been missing from home for over a week. Long Beach PD has the case. The case number is shown there too," the sweatshirted investigator in shorts told the bored and utterly uninterested desk sergeant.

"Yeah, sonny boy, they'll get 'em," the heavy and crusty cop growled as he took the fliers and tossed them carelessly into the half-full wire tray on his desk, picking up the ringing telephone.

Steve knew there was nothing more to say or do here and turned to leave. "Hope she doesn't turn forty before the beach patrol gets those fliers," he shouted over his shoulder at the dense blue shape. No reply or nasty look. Santa Monica's finest is not going to be making any kind of effort, thought Steve, so I guess I'd better keep working the beach and surfer crowd myself.

Santa Monica's Muscle Beach fronted the sunny strand adjacent to the old-timey carousel, run down amusement park, and fishing pier that jutted out a city block long into the bay.

A crowd of Mid-western Debbies and Darryls parked themselves along the strand like white whales necklaced with shiny, black Kodak Brownies, staring, pointing, and clicking away at the deeply tanned bodybuilders and gymnasts doing their thing: aerial flips, human pyramids, pumping big iron, and undulating abdominal exhibitions.

Always a few Bruces about too, ogling speedos and wishing. The flat beach sand near the boardwalk was pockmarked with scooped-out shallow pits where the sand pumpers had been lying face down. One hand in the crotch, eyeing the multitude of cleavage, buns, and breasts baking in the sun or on a stroll. Pretty obvious.

The local fuzz ignored the solo sex but when the lifeguards spotted one they walked up to him and kicked some sand, telling the habitués to "Fuck off and don't come back." A new seasonal crop of pumpers descended on the ever-popular Santa Monica beach like a flock of pigeons until chased off again to inhabit other beaches.

Farther south, at Venice, the boardwalk populace was more eclectic. Strange looking loonies, a darker racial mix, gypsy look-alikes, and longhairs were the norm—not the exception. The local surfers there couldn't care less who inhabited the boardwalk.

The chalk people's favorite gawking place held a very slim possibility of a Gloria sighting. Steve gave the tourist area a pass, except to see Joe.

Joe Gold wasn't part of the surfing set, nor was he a gymnast. Joe was strictly a well-conditioned body builder who enjoyed exhibiting his splendid torso at the beach. His body was his business card. A six-foot frame with the bronze color and sheen of a well-basted tom turkey—without an ounce of fat on him.

Over a decade in the warm California sun while basting his bod with cocoa butter and baby oil had transformed his pale Polish frame into the epitome of the Muscle Beach Man. Steve knew Joe's nephew, Ray "Sunny" Gold, from the Redondo Beach surfing crowd, and figured he could use the "Sunny's Buddy" angle on Uncle Joe.

Gold was sitting posture perfect on a strand bench, effortlessly doing ten-pound reps with a pair of chromed barbells—pump, pump, pump. He was now in his thirties and a sensationally sculpted specimen who would have looked great in marble. "Mr. Gold? I'm Steve Lund, a friend of your nephew, Sunny. Do you have a couple of minutes? I'm not selling anything, just have something important to ask you," Steve announced to the bronzed work of living art.

Gold kept rhythmically pumping the ten-pound barbells without missing a beat. Steve thought maybe repping iron kept Joe's juices circulating like a Signal Hill oil well pumping crude through a myriad of iron pipes. Joe looked the surfer up and down, squinting at the shaggy young man clad in a sleeveless sweatshirt, faded denim shorts, and shod in zoris.

"Yeah. You look like another one of those shagnasty surfers. Just like that surf bum nephew of mine. I can spare you a few minutes of gab, but remember, our bodies are always aging—going to seed every second. No rest periods or time off for Joe Gold or Charles Atlas! Gotta keep in top form or I'm out of business. Nobody pays an out-of-shape slob to teach them bodybuilding and fitness, right, Mr. Lund?" Mr. Muscle Beach stated emphatically while endlessly moving iron.

"You're right. You have the look of a classic Greek statue—with a Polish mug. Keep pumping, Joe. I just want to show you a flier on a missing girl." Steve held out two flier sheets. "Here's her photo and details about her, plus the phone numbers to contact me or her father. There would be a grand in it for you. If you see her, call us."

Joe Gold took the fliers with one brown paw, while keeping one chrome barbell rhythmically going up and down in the other. "Nope. Haven't seen her. Not a bad looking girl, but she could use some definition work, especially in the legs. If I do see her around, I'll give her dad a call. Don't want your bounty money, Lund. It would be dirty."

"That's fine, Mr. Gold. It's your choice. I'm sure her father would really appreciate your help," the chastened detective replied.

"Your allotted time is up, Mr. Lund. Hope you find your missing girl. I'll watch for her. And tell that surf bum nephew of mine to come on by and see me sometime."

"I'll tell him. Going to Venice now anyway," replied Steve as he endured Joe's power grip. He headed back to the Santa Monica Pier, shaking some feeling back into his right hand. He wanted to interview the security patrol and amusement ride employees.

The large black and yellow sign over the entrance to the pier—Santa Monica Yacht Harbor—was amusing. There were no yachts to be seen and no harbor in sight. Steve left a few fliers at the business office and talked to the uninterested ticket takers at the rides. A dry run. "Guess I'm not much of a sleuth—can't find a single yacht or even the supposed harbor right here under my nose!"

After a burger basket with fries and a cold Oly on the strand below the pier, Steve drove south down bayside Ocean Avenue to check out the early afternoon surf at the Venice, Manhattan, and Redondo beaches. He stopped briefly at the surfboard shop owned by Dale Velzy and Hap Jacobs in Venice, near the pier, to find out if they had any information on the elusive Gloria or a lead on the yellow stick that Dale had shaped and sold to her.

Their funky shop was a combination of walk-in sales in front and "factory" in the back, where the duo supposedly handcrafted a surfboard to their customer's style and proficiency. Dale or Hap would size up the client and could usually produce "just the right one" from their available stock in the racks, or shape and glass one to order in a couple of days. "Same price off the rack or made to order. Same amount of work to make 'em," Dale explained.

Sometimes that custom-made board was sold to someone else by the time the customer who placed the order came back to pick it up, so again it would be a few more days, but well worth the wait—and no point in bitching, either. Hap and Dale burned the midnight oil to catch up on orders whenever the surf was up, which was often enough. Surf days, shape nights, was the credo they lived by.

Lund found Dale in the shop out back where he was roughing out a board from a laminated balsa-redwood blank. "Hi, Dale. How's biz?" he asked.

"Busier than a bull rider in action. What can I do for you, Lund? Ready to order a new fat-tail stick?" queried the balsa-dust-covered shaper.

"I'll be ready for one in about a month. Right now I'm trying to track down a Long Beach girl, a customer of yours, actually. She's missing." Steve handed Velzy a Gloria flier.

"Yeah. I remember making a board for that babe. A greenhorn," he recalled. "Haven't seen either one since she bought it here in May. There was a man with her when she picked up her board. An older guy, gentleman with glasses. Her dad, I guess. Didn't say much, but he paid."

"Yeah, probably her father, but thanks for the tip. Mind if I put one of these fliers about her up in your sales room window out front? Some surfer might have seen her or your yellow stick."

"Sure. Go right ahead," Dale shouted over the buzz of the electric sander as he worked a surfboard balsa blank.

"See you back here in a month then, when you get tired of trying a snap-turn on that big ol' Peterson log of yours."

"Deal," Steve replied as he walked out into the display area to tape a flier inside the front window.

Next step? He still had the prime surfer towns of Venice, El Segundo, Manhattan, Hermosa, and Redondo to search. Fifteen miles of wide and white sandy beaches, with myriads of knob kneed boarders to make inquiries to about Gloria. Dozens of coffee shops and diners to check. He decided to first hit Venice and track down Ray "Sunny" Gold and just paper the rest of the beaches later with fliers along the strand. He could do a more thorough canvass of them after scouring the Orange and San Diego beaches.

Venice—the salty, crusty, and worn stuccoed edge of L.A.—was an eclectic seaside town slowly decaying, exfoliating, and rusting away. Once a real estate developer's California Dream, complete with canals, it had turned sour and seedy soon after the Crash of 1929.

Cheap rents for the musty, pastel-pink stucco apartments that invariably grew varicolored mold in the closet on tenants' clothes and shoes attracted a conglomerate of low-wage earners, drifters, and pseudo-artists. The Venice beachfront was also a prime residential location for unemployed surfers, usually stuffing four or more buddies into a dingy seaside "villa" studio pad. Even a dark and dank garage would do for a cheap or free place to flop with your board, an old mattress, and a sandy beach dog.

Venice looked like the perfect place in which to get lost forever, just like Uncle Bert had said, thought Steve, parking his dusty Ford on seedy Brooks Court, just off Main Street, a block from the beach and strand. A grinning and quite-dead black cat at the curb line was the first to greet him to Venice's beach community as he stepped out of his truck. Damn near stepped right on that flyblown pussycat, grimaced the visitor.

The acrid stench from the rotting and dank debris in the gutter traveled up his nose like a dark brown stain, mingling with rank odors of stale beer and tobacco butts that emanated from the musty beer bars lining both sides of the narrow side street and overpowered the pungent sea air.

A shapeless gray transient stumbled aimlessly out of a trash-filled alleyway where detritus lay in windblown heaps like banks of dirty snow. His pants were stained with urine, some of it still wet; his untied shoelaces dragging along like dead angleworms. The vag was grinning at the untested detective, showing ragged yellowed stumps rotting in a grizzled Kelly-the-Clown mouth.

No use asking anything of the old rummy, reasoned Steve, as an incoherent rambling reply would surely be the only thing forthcoming. The detective pulled a crumpled dollar bill from his pocket, wordlessly shoved a Gloria flier and the buck into the wino's shaky palm, and kept walking towards the beach strand. The old fart stood staring at the dollar bill and the paper in his hand.

Stepping onto the Venice strand and into the bright beach glare was like suddenly emerging onto a funky movie set. The onshore breeze gusted fresh and clean on his face. Steve inhaled deeply, glad to be away from the side street stink.

Steve marveled at the mix of scatological words and graphics inscribed with charcoal fragments on the knee-high concrete barricade separating the beach from the walkway that resembled inscriptions by ancient Egyptian graffiti artists on tomb walls.

He found Ray 'Sunny' Gold sprawled next to the low concrete wall of the strand, along with a pair of browned boarders who were sunning themselves like six-foot bronze lizards. Three scarred surfboards, crusted with wax and sand, were racked up against the low wall on the beach side. All three of the young surfers looked similar, six-foot-tall with shoulder-length, bleached-out, yellowed hair and lithe browned bodies clad only in cutoffs.

"Hey, Stevie! Whatcha doin' ova' here in Venass town? Get tired of the piddling surf and butt ugly girls down in Huntington?" ragged Joe Gold's young nephew as he sat up to greet Steve.

"Nothin' that desperate, Sunny. Just trying to locate a fine young water maiden before she goes bad over here bayside," replied Steve.

"We like 'em bad, bayside!" laughed one of Ray's bronze buddies.

"Stay away from our stuff. We're not into sharing," joked the third member of the locals, with a friendly scowl.

"You bums have the wrong idea. I'm not over here to hook any Manhattan mermaids. Next time over this way tho', watch it! You'd better hide your keepers. Take a squint at this flier and no horny comments. This brown-eyed mermaid is missing, and I think she may have washed ashore around here. Name's Gloria, but who knows, she could be calling herself something else. There's a grand in cash for the lowly beach rat who spots her and calls it in to me, if it turns out to be her, that is. She might just love riding your teeny-weenie, two-footer bunny waves on her new Velzy, here at Venass or Redondo," Steve taunted.

"Maybe we'll just net your water sprite and hold out for a larger ransom. She looks on paper to be worth at least twenty bucks a pound, not ten as advertised, and we could use that new Velzy ourselves," smiled Sunny.

"Better cash her in for the guaranteed grand. You know the old saying about a mermaid in hand. Don't get greedy. She may just vanish again and you three bozos would be SOL. Fuck around with this fish and you deal with me, a pissed-off father, and the Long Beach fuzz," cautioned Steve with a small smile.

"The boys and I were just jerking your chain, Stevie. We'll keep a sharp lookout for your precious Gloria and 'specially for the Velzy. Good luck with the fishing. Let's all head out and catch a few sets. Rights are breaking, and the swells are a steady four feet or better. A rideable wave only peaks once, you know, so let's go get our share now. Maybe your mermaid's out right now, waiting for you to show."

"Yeah, OK. See you bums in ten," promised Steve. He trotted back to the surf wagon to retrieve his board and while there stealthily pulled from his roof rack a half-dozen comic-strip tubes for the troops.

It felt good to slice through the incoming breakers and finally get outside, beyond the cresting waves. I'm going to get out of sync and lose my surfing skills after a month of this bounty hunter crap, thought Steve. Probably just a big goddamn snipe hunt, this Gloria search business. I shouldn't have taken on this girl-in-a-haystack fiasco. A fruitless fucking waste of my surfing time—and undoubtedly I look like a dumbfuck to my surfing buddies. They will be begging me to track down their girlfriend's lost toy poodle for ten bucks, grumbled Steve. Screw it! I'm taking this whole afternoon off to surf with Sunny and his horny louts.

He stroked hard into a rising four-footer, quickly stood, and slashed across the thick right shoulder, right hand trailing lightly in the hollow green curl at his backside. Gonna be a bitchin' day, thought Steve.

The awesome afternoon surf session lasted until the four-thirty wind and chop arrived, as usual. The lack of daily surfing sessions may have begun to dull his edge as a proficient waterman, but he felt newly recharged and energized, ready to resume his search.

He reminded Sunny to check in with his Uncle Joe. "Think I will tomorrow," said Sunny. "Uncle Joe is always good for a few bucks, too. Thanks for the local comics, ol' bud. See ya latah."

Steve left the Venass Boys back at the strand wall, took a cold shower next to the public restrooms, and went to find a pay phone. He dialed Mr. Hess, hoping for some good news. Hess sounded depressed. The dad had checked every day with the LBPD, phoned Gloria's girlfriends again, and diligently scanned the local beach newspapers for any leads. Nothing.

"It's still early in the chase," Steve told him, "so just keep plugging away at your end and I'll do the same. Something will turn up that leads to her, or she'll come back home, you'll see. We don't have any bad news, so that's the good news, isn't it? I'm headed back home now. I'm going to try to make an appointment for tomorrow with Gloria's shrink, Dr. Grayson. She might have some insight about her patient's disappearance and what her mental state might have been prior to that Sunday night. I'll be in touch with you soon."

"Thanks for the encouragement, Steve. I do feel we will find her, but I doubt that Dr. Grayson will be of much help. I know Gloria is OK, somewhere. Call me soon then," replied the distressed but somewhat resigned father.

Steve drove home and was fortunate to hit on mom's pot roast with potatoes night, since these days she only cooked once a week—for the week. After dinner the stuffed gumshoe took a long hot shower, washed clothes, poked everything into the dryer and hit the sack early. Sleeping in until eight-thirty the next morning, he wolfed down three hot-sauced scrambled eggs with toast and cups of black coffee. The apprentice detective phoned the pensioned professional, Uncle Bert, and filled him in on the search so far—skipping the part about the roll in the hay at Malibu.

"Don't rush and you won't have to comb an area twice," Uncle Bert advised. "Take your time. A solid lead will turn up, I'll bet on it. It sounds like you may have that bloodhound instinct, Steve."

Steve called Bill Bristow at 9:15 AM and woke him up. "Billy B, it's Steve. How's the job goin'? Any problems crop up that I will need to know about?"

Sleepy Bill answered, "No *problema*, Steve. Funny, most customers don't even ask if you're dead or alive, so I don't tell 'em nuthin'. They just want their goods delivered ASAP. What do you want me to do with the cash I've collected? I don't want to hang onto this large chunk of your loot."

"Just motor over and leave it with my mom early this evening. Once a week is OK. Just stuff it in a grocery sack. She knows where I keep an empty suitcase. I'll count the two-week's take and bank it when I get back from San Diego. I have a pretty fair idea of what the total should be, don't you?"

"Sure. I wouldn't short you, Steve. This is a slam dunk winner of a job!" said Bill.

"I think we can make a business arrangement which will be mutually profitable in the long run. I'm tired of a seven-night-a-week job anyway. If you want to think it over, we can talk when this search for Gloria thing is over. It'll only last a few more weeks one way or another."

"Sounds like a plan. It's easy money but it's also hard on my sex life, working seven nights a week," said Bill.

"Your love life's gonna vastly improve a few weeks from now with chunks of cash to blow on your bimbos," replied Steve, "so for the moment just play it straight and cool. Gotta go, so *ciao* for now."

It was nine-forty-five when Steve phoned Dr. Grayson's office, and by intimating that his call was a "police matter" regarding Gloria Hess and insisting that he must talk to Dr. Grayson personally, he finally succeeded in bullshitting his way past the receptionist to the doctor herself.

"This is Steve Lund, Dr. Grayson. I'd like to meet with you sometime today for a few minutes concerning Gloria Hess. She's missing, as you know. I've been employed by her father, Dieter Hess, to find her and would appreciate a short interview with you concerning her mental state when she disappeared."

"Oh. So you are a modern-day bounty hunter, and not associated with the police after all, correct, Mr. Lund? I could not possibly divulge confidential patient information to you concerning Miss Hess. Besides, I'm booked solid all this week."

"As I said, Dr. Grayson, I was hired by Mr. Hess to locate his daughter, not to drag her home by the hair or in handcuffs to collect bounty money. I'm not asking for your patient's confidential couch confessions, just your insight on why she might've taken a hike. Perhaps you've heard from Gloria since she disappeared? Her father just wants to know that she is OK, not to lock her in a castle and throw away the key. If you are booked during business hours, I could take you to Russell's for lunch. They have great burgers and peach pie. It's just a few blocks up Atlantic from your office. You don't have a lunch engagement, do you?"

"To answer your first question, no, I haven't heard from Gloria. But all right, Mr. Lund, against my better judgment, you can pick me up at my office at 11:45, sharp. I must be back here by one. We can *informally* discuss Miss Hess during lunch. Is that acceptable?"

"That would be perfect. Thank you. I'll be at your office 11:45 sharp."

Appointment confirmed, he got his old reliable rustbucket fueled, watered, and oiled. A quick hose job of a Mexican carwash blasted off most of the salty grime and sand from his trip north. No more time to goof off, Steve reminded himself, as he replenished the bagged grass supply from the hidden stash in the garage. It was about 11:00 AM by the time Steve had repacked the panel truck. Dressed in his best, nearly new, black polo shirt and a clean pair of faded 501 Levis, he hustled down to Bixby Knolls to make that "11:45 sharp" meeting.

Helen Grayson, M.D., didn't look a day over thirty, more than likely under that, to the surprise of the young detective. Curvy and petite, her auburn hair was pulled back into a spiral swirl, gray eyes peeked out behind tortoiseshell glasses, and there was no hint of makeup. She looked sharp and professional in her beige linen skirt suit and ivory silk blouse. No jewelry, no ring on the left hand. Strictly straight arrow on the surface and all business nine-to-five.

"Didn't expect such a fox," smiled the admiring detective as he escorted the svelte doctor to his bread wagon parked on the street in front of her office complex.

She didn't blink or change expressions as he opened the squeaky passenger-side door of his rustbucket. His attire of polo shirt, Levis, and *huaraches* didn't seem to bother her either. Dr. Grayson had suspected, when making the lunch appointment over the phone, she was dealing with an unconventional young man.

"I don't transmogrify into a fox until after dark," the mind doctor said with a slight smile.

"Sounds fine to me, Doctor. You're certainly not a reincarnation of Chimera."

"Are you a student of Greek mythology in your spare time, Mr. Lund?"

"I've read some of it. Homer's *Ulysses* and *The Odyssey* make for great beach reading. Poseidon's my favorite since he is the god of the sea. The Trojan War was fought over a beautiful woman, as you well know. By the way, did your parents name you after Helen of Troy?"

"I might be *her* reincarnation. I hope not that of Chimera, the fire-breathing monster," Dr. Grayson replied with a playful hiss through her teeth.

It was a quick run up Atlantic Boulevard, Steve parked at a meter, and they took seats at the counter of the ever-busy Russell's. They each ordered the house's famous four-napkin burger, and Steve added a plate of hash browns to share.

"I only met Dieter Hess once, at the commencement of my sessions with Gloria, eighteen months ago. He seemed quite reserved and only just tolerating of my treatment of his daughter's depression. I don't believe Mr. Hess thought I could bring her out of it, but she was recently making very good progress, adjusting to the loss of her mother. Her mother's death was very traumatic, as you might imagine, and after the tragedy Gloria did not seem to have anyone else to help her to heal her emotional wounds and fears. Gloria was making headway, learning to cope and to manage her melancholy and sadness.

"If I may say so, and again, quite confidentially, Mr. Hess also had his daughter on such a short leash, like the owner of a virgin French poodle. Boys taking her on a date had to tell him where they were going and were forewarned she had a strict, eleven-thirty curfew. No exceptions. Even on her high school prom night, Gloria explained to me, she had to be home by 11:30 sharp, which caused her some consternation and embarrassment among her peers. Something else was bothering Gloria after her mother, Grace, died. She would never tell me what it was, but it had to do with her father and mother. She did assure me that there were no incestuous situations with him. I think she left home to punish her father for something, though. That's my professional inclination. Please don't share what I said to you with Mr. Hess. He wouldn't like it," she said.

"Don't worry, I won't. That's an interesting speculation. There probably was something besides living with an overprotective father that caused the nymph to sprout wings and fly away," said Steve.

"I have to be back to my office in a few minutes, so shall we go? Thank you for the lunch. I hope our discussion will provide you with some insight into her mental condition. She is pretty stable now, not a candidate for suicide in my book. I don't know if any of this will help you though."

"You need all the numbers of the combination to open the mind's vault, don't you agree?" declared the detective, as he escorted the shapely Dr. Grayson out of the restaurant and to his lowly surf wagon. She simply nodded in affirmation.

As Steve thanked the mind detector for her time and insights, he asked her with a sly smile, "If I decide to go fox hunting at the end of the month, when the moon is full, do you think my quarry would be a willing participant?"

"I doubt you would be very successful in your pursuit of the elusive vixen while riding a mangy gray nag and wearing beach sandals. Vixens would prefer to be pursued by well-dressed gentlemen riding on thoroughbreds. Don't you agree?"

"That is a succinct way of expressing your viewpoint. I will have to review the hunt and the quarry from that perspective, won't I?"

"Good afternoon, Ulysses. I hope your quest of Gloria is successful. Please let me know when your odyssey is concluded and she is found, hopefully, safe and sound."

"I will make it one of my personal goals to fulfill your request, Dr. Grayson, and relate the exciting details of the quest to you in person over lunch or dinner."

"Foxes are always hungry. Keep in touch, with your progress," she said, touching his tanned arm with her fingertips. "And you can call me Helen."

The foxhunter trotted back to his Ford and headed down Atlantic Boulevard for Highway 1 and points farther south. Do I really want to go to all that effort and expense, he wondered, to pursue and capture Dr. Foxxe? I'd have to rent a new ragtop and buy some dress threads to take up the chase. I'll bet the moonlight transformation would be something else. Maybe that pot of gold is at the end of the Gloria rainbow; I'll just have to chase it down.

Southbound on Highway 1, yet again. The searcher rolled his rusty bucket into the graveled parking lot at TURCS, a surfer-biker beer bar adjacent to the highway at Sunset Beach. One-twenty in the afternoon and thirsty for a mug or two of TURCS' cold Brew of the Week on tap—high octane stuff! The dive was a good place to post a Gloria flier and fill in Lloyd, the daytime barkeep, on the bounty angle.

TURCS was a small, weather-beaten joint, with faded-yellow stucco and an ancient, green tarpapered roof. It had a previous life as an auto repair shop. This bar was not a good place to take your date, unless she was drunk or liked to go slumming among nefarious hog bikers, low lifers, and skuzzy surfers. Cheap, cold tap beer was TURCS' magnetic liquid attraction, nothing else.

The dim bar was customer sparse on the early summer Monday afternoon, even with the sun out and hot. Steve slid onto a worn, wooden swivel stool at the scarred mahogany bar, one seat away from a heavyset biker. The outlaw was prickly cactus bald and wearing oily black leather pants and boots, his chunky torso clad in a sleeveless, swastika-backed leather vest. The oversized hog rider had multi-colored cheap tattoos on both hammy pink arms. One distinctive tattoo etched on his right biceps was a misspelled phrase in black ink: DEATH BEFOR DISHONOR. The stubble-faced biker glowered at the newcomer with a hooded brow and malevolent stare. Trouble, no doubt.

Steve ignored the Neanderthal's stink eye as Lloyd set down "the usual": an ice cold, dark amber, pint of the Brew of the Week and two pickled eggs.

"'Lo, Lloyd. Quiet in here this afternoon for such an attractive, upscale place. Take a squint at this flier for me. The girl is missing, and there's a nice chunk of change coming for whoever helps locate her for me," the surfer informed his gray T-shirt clad, middle-aged, ponytailed barman, as he laid two Gloria fliers face up on the bar's counter.

The big biker reached over with a scarred, meaty fist and plucked a flier off the counter. He squinted at it briefly, with a wicked smile. "Woo wee, just a grand for that nice sweet cherry? I could rake in way over a grand, easy, with that tender pussy at just one Mogul gangbang!" snorted the tough-talking scooter jockey.

The boarder coolly drained the remaining half of his cold draft, wrapping his fist through the mug's heavy glass handle and gently rested the empty glass on the counter. In one quick motion Steve swept the beer mug off the bar and spun around to his left, right arm fully extended. The heavy glass weapon caught the foul-mouthed biker flush on the nose and forehead. SMACK! Right between his surprised blue eyes. The tattooed ogre lurched heavily backward off the barstool and thudded hard on the tiled floor, like two hundred pounds of wet cement. Splat. "Biker out of Order," casually remarked Steve, as he retrieved the Gloria flier from the floor and handed it back to Lloyd. Nobody in the place made a move or a sound.

"See ya, Lloyd. Sorry about the cracked mug," called out the apologetic surfer as he stepped around the prostrate pink and black form, careful not to step in the nosebleed mess. Leaving a Lincoln on the bar for the beer, eggs, and badly cracked beer mug, he strolled out the front door into the bright sun. Might as well catch a few quick waves at Huntington Pier, he thought, cranking up the Ford's loose V-8 and rolling out of the parking lot onto PCH.

Determined to not miss any surfing spots, no matter how unlikely, Gloria's searcher pulled off along the busy highway at Tom's shack on Tin Can Beach, two miles south of Sunset Beach and TURCS. Tin Can was blanketed with rusty beer cans and discarded wine bottles, the cumulative effect of too many years as a sadly neglected stretch of California seashore. Wild beach parties with huge scrap wood bonfires lit up the beach sky at night, all year long, year after year.

A few semi-permanent squatters lived on the wind-swept, rusty expanse of sandy beach. Makeshift shacks of old bottles and driftwood, topped with cardboard and plywood scraps, were scattered haphazardly along the five-mile stretch of ill-used beach between Sunset and Huntington. Most squatters had cleared their own homestead beachfront of glass and rusty cans, making a pathway from shack to highway. Rumor had it that California State Parks had big plans to evict all the beach's residents and sanitize the five-mile stretch for a new ocean side recreational and RV complex.

Steve rousted old Tom out of his bottles-plywood-driftwood palace that was half buried in sand. A Dakota prairie sod house transplanted onto the littered strand of Southern California beach.

"Tom! Yo, Tom!" the visitor hollered through the Bandini burlap-bag door. "I've got some brew and some grass out here for you, if you're interested, which I know you are, so get your sandy old ass out here."

"Hold on, sonny, hold on!" came a gravelly voice from within the dank, makeshift hovel. Tom stumbled unsteadily out into the bright sunlight, as if he hadn't seen sun in days. His scraggly clothes and crusty beard made him a casting agent's dream for Robinson Crusoe, and he scratched himself earnestly at the crotch.

"Well, well. If it ain't Surfer Steve. What brings you by to see old Tom? The surf has been kinda puny 'round here the past few days," the beachcomber cackled.

"Need your help, Tom," said Steve, as he handed the grizzled old fellow a six-pack and a baggie of weed. "I want you to pass out these fliers to all the squats and surfers from Sunset to the Bluffs. There's a girl from Long Beach who's missing, and I've been hired to find her. You can make yourself a thousand bucks—or split it if you and your beach bum pals can locate her for me."

"Well, Bud, it will take some mighty trudging up and down this dumpy beach, but I'll give it a try. It's gonna take more than one six-pack of beer to do it, though. How 'bout some quarts? It ain't likely a lone surfer girl would be beaching it here, is it?"

"No, Tom. It isn't likely, but who knows what a ditzy babe might do, especially when she doesn't want to be found. Check out all the beach shacks and pass out those fliers. I'll bring you a couple of cold quarts in a few days. Call me, collect, if you see or hear anything about her and I'll be here, pronto."

"Just like an old bounty hunter in a Zane Gray western, right, young Steve?" remarked the aged beach denizen. He wrenched open a can of Schlitz and took a long swig.

"Guess you're right about that, old man. Are you worried they're going to kick you all out and turn this into a deluxe RV park?" Steve asked.

"I'm staying put until the State brings in the bulldozers and demolishes my shack. Where am I gonna go, anyway? I'll just find some *arroyo* down the coast to live at, since I can't hardly move farther west," the old geezer said wistfully.

See ya soon, then," said the searcher as he turned and ambled back to the highway.

Steve papered the surfer cars, vans, and wagons parked on the Bluffs along the highway with Gloria fliers. Most boarders were out riding, not on the beach. Viewed from the roadside edge of the bluff, the waves looked small and ragged in the light choppy sea.

It was four and therefore ample justification to stop at Dwight's for a couple of Jack Clapp's great hot dogs smothered in spicy, red gunk, topped with a handful of chopped onion. The whitewashed, plywood dog stand was planted smack on the sand, just south of the Huntington Pier. Jack's dad, Dwight, had started the business in 1932, and Jack began working there at ten, renting the umbrellas.

That was twenty years past. Clean air and plenty to eat were good enough reasons to stay, according to "Hefty Jack."

"Gimme two dogs with extra gunk and onion, will ya, Jack? I lugged a couple of cold brews along since you can't sell booze on the beach. Want one?"

"Sure, Steve. Crack me open a can while I fix your dogs. An even trade," smiled the pudgy owner.

"I want to post one of these fliers of Gloria Hess here at your stand. Remember her? She's been missing for about two weeks. She might show up around here with her Velzy board and green Chevy wagon."

"The body looks familiar but I don't always remember the face," laughed Jack as he swapped the dogs for beer. "Haven't seen her or that stick for over two weeks. I'll give you a buzz if I do, though, bet on it. Be careful holding onto those two messy dogs. With all that sauce on them, they might squirm right out of your grip."

"Thanks, Big Jack. Think I'll take a flying leap in the Pond after I polish off these doggies. I'm heading down the coast to San Diego. I'll check in with you again on my way back."

After a quick running dive into the surf to wash off hot dog gunk and bodysurf a few powerful shore breaks, the salty detective showered off at the beachside restroom. Still wet, he climbed back into the bread truck and headed to Kenny's in Newport Beach where he was always welcome. Kenny Estep and his three surfer-student cronies lived in a four-man, upper-level duplex on the Balboa peninsula. Huntington Beach and the Bluffs were just five miles north up Highway 1; Newport's broad beach was just outside their door; and San Onofre's perfect breaks were less than twenty miles south. Location, location, location, as real estate brokers say.

Their Bal beach pad was strictly utilitarian. Bunk beds and faded canvas camp chairs on sandy wooden floors. Paper plates and plastic utensils stacked on a purloined California State Park wooden picnic bench. Nothing to bother washing up except the occasional stewpot or fry pan. One plywood-paneled wall of the living/dining room was stacked solid, floor to ceiling, with beer cans—two deep. Kenny's aunt owned the building so the surfer-scholars were careful not to trash the place or unduly aggravate the neighbors or local fuzz.

Orange Coast Junior College—the JC—was conveniently situated for surfer-students, only two miles from the Pacific Ocean. You couldn't find a more ideal location for a combo of surf and college. The easygoing Fifties faculty and students were just mellowing out in Lotusland. No need for Kenny and the boys to go elsewhere on a spring Easter break like most college students. They were living the summer resort life at Balboa all year round on a perpetual spring break.

"Hey! Little Stevie," hollered Kenny from his seldom-used kitchen. "How goes the big chase, Bird Dog? Catch up with Gloria or any strange stuff? How 'bout a brewski or two to settle the road dust?"

"Sho' 'nuff I'll take one. I've got a few more in the rustbucket outside. Glad to see you're lookin' so good. No sniff of Gloria so far, but I ran into some sweet stuff up in Malibu, thanks to Leo and Larry. Surf was humpin' there, too. I spotted some fine point breaks up the coast— Rincon was cranking out four-footers like a wave machine.

I papered the north coast with fliers and had a few fungi-induced false sightings of my quarry. Other than that, nothing much on the elusive Miss G search to report. How goes it with you, Ken?"

"Can't bitch. Who'd listen, anyway? Swells have been no more than threes, but the fridge has cold beer and sex-hungry summer tourists have been warming up my bunk pretty regular this week. Did you bring along some of your primo Mexican pot? I'm getting low."

"I'll share what I have along, old bud. You don't need a kilo since you gave up peddling dope, right?"

Estep stood at six-two and two hundred. His many years spent on the beach and in the ocean had turned his shaggy mane yellow and his XL frame tanned to teakwood. The ladies quickly fell for his innocent, brown Golden Lab eyes. Broken-Nose Estep had been whacked by his own spiraling surfboard after a nearly fatal error in judgment flipped his errant stick out of a breaking wave and high into the air. Lucky for Kenny it smacked him butt-end first. He considered his off-centered schnoz the mark of a true waterman.

Kenny was the nutcase wave ripper while Steve had a smooth, hang-loose approach to boarding. Two distinct styles on a wave, who's to say which made the better waterman? Estep, master of the vertical drop-in and bottom-turn snaps left and right, or Lund, shooting the curl, crouching low in the pipe, stomping hard on the tail to exit up and over the fading wave?

"Say, Mr. Bounty Hunter, remember that *chubasco* storm that came barreling in at San Onofre and Dana Point last year, bringing cresting fifteen-feet-plus powerhouses? Awesome. Never seen anything like that liquid locomotive before or since. Wild and wooly rides! That was some max-imum session, wasn't it, bro'?"

"Yeah. Those spitting barrels were massive and thick as mud. Two solid days, sunup to sundown. Bitchin', just bitchin' off the Point. We'll do it again when another *chubasco* hits the coast, maybe next spring," said Steve. "Hey, OK with you if I make a quick phone call to Long Beach? It's 6:30 and I'd better call Gloria's father."

Dieter Hess answered Steve's call on the first ring, sounding panicky and as if he'd been waiting by the phone. "Steve! The Santa Monica lifeguards pulled a girl out of the ocean, around noon today. She drowned while surfing off the beach there—got caught in a rip current. I saw a five o'clock news broadcast about it on the TV. The police have not identified her yet, according to the broadcast. I called the Santa Monica Police, but they wouldn't release any in-formation or details over the phone to me. Should I drive up there right now? Oh God! What if the girl is Gloria!" he cried frantically.

"Slow down, Mr. Hess," Steve interrupted. "You just sit tight. I'll drive to Santa Monica right away—it will only take me an hour or so. Stay right where you are, at home. Chances are it isn't Gloria. There are probably a hundred or more girls on surfboards in Santa Monica Bay on any summer day. Let me handle this. I'll call you from Santa Monica as soon as I find out who she is."

"Hurry, Steve, please. I can't stand the thought of my daughter in some morgue, dead. Please call me just as soon as you can. I'll wait by this phone and keep the line clear for your call," the anxious father pleaded.

"I'm leaving Newport Beach right now," assured Steve. "Keep watching the news on TV. I'll call you back when I find out—give me an hour or so to get there."

Steve grabbed a cold slice of pizza from Kenny's fridge and said he should be back in a few hours. He pointed his trusty rustbucket northward up Highway 1 and was soon traveling at seventy, a can of cold beer stashed between his legs and his right foot mashed on the gas.

His AM radio tuned to KRKD, he tapped the steering wheel as DJ Jack Nemo laid down a succession of hits: "Big Man," by The Four Preps, Duane Eddy's "Rebel 'Rouser," The Crests' "My Juanita," and Sam Cooke's number 1 hit "You Send Me." The Ford sailed through the beach towns, Long Beach, Redondo, and Hermosa, blowing off yellow lights—even red ones that looked makeable. A few close calls but no flashing red lights or cop car sirens on his ass. There were panic skid marks, horns blaring, and a few fist-shaking truck drivers who swore at the weaving ancient bread truck as it sailed precariously through the South Bay intersections. It still took an hour and fifteen to lead-foot it from Newport to the Santa Monica Police Station.

Cold day in hell before I try something like that again, Steve grumbled to himself as he parked the steaming, over-heated old Ford. The forlorn vehicle groaned in protest. He jogged quickly across the street and into the police station.

The night-shift desk cop was a young, red-haired Irishman with a florid face, big nose, and jutting chin. The young detective pulled out a Gloria flier and laid it on the counter in front of the newly minted officer of the law. "I'm Steve Lund, officer. I am on the case of a missing girl, Gloria Hess from Long Beach. I heard on the news that a young girl drowned in the Santa Monica surf today. Can you tell me if a positive ID has been made on her yet?" stated Steve in his best private-investigator voice. The Irish rookie picked up the flier and studied both sides, reading all the details, then picked up his telephone and dialed.

"Susan. Do you have an ID on that young lassie that drowned in our ocean today?" the redhead asked while staring hard at the young gumshoe. "Fine. Thank you, Susan. Nope, not your lassie. The dead girl's name wasn't Gloria. That's all I can tell you, officially. If you want any further details, buy the *Times* in the morning, or come back tomorrow and talk to Sergeant Maloney, my uncle. I don't know who you work for, laddie, but it isn't the Long Beach Police Department, now is it? Not in that getup you're wearing— cutoff sweatshirt and surfer trunks," stated the skeptical Irishman.

"That's all I need to know, Officer. Thanks for the info. Here's a dozen or so fliers for your beach patrol. I hope they get them this time." It was eight-thirty when he called Mr. Hess with the good news, all things considered, that the Gloria search was back on schedule.

It was still early enough to refuel his much-abused bread wagon and make the drive back to Kenny's pad in Balboa for the night. This time, however, he took it slow and easy down PCH and showed up at ten-thirty, dog tired from his urban road race. Steve stopped on the highway near the turnoff to the Balboa peninsula and sprang for two pepperoni pizzas and a couple of Schlitz six-packs. When he got to Kenny's Bal house, everyone greeted him at the door with cheers.

Steve was still sleeping at nine AM, top bunk in the extra rack, when Kenny shook the iron bedstead and almost rocked his visiting buddy out on the floor. "Phone call for you, Rip. Some guy says it's important. Hit the deck, Bud."

It was Dieter Hess again. Steve had left Kenny's phone number with him. Hess had spotted a Velzy surfboard for sale in the *Newport Bay News*. The ad was now two days old, due to the newspaper mailing time and Dieter's forgetting to mention it during last night's excitement about the girl drowning in Santa Monica. Hess had tried calling the ad's number at eight AM but no answer. "Is there some way to get an address and name with only a telephone number?" Mr. Hess asked.

"Sure," Steve told him. "There's a crisscross directory that will give me a street address and usually a listed name. I'll stop at the local library this morning and check it out. Good work!"

Hollering "See ya later," at the doorway, the still-groggy private eye left Estep's and drove back to the PCH. He pulled into an empty, front-row slot at the Three Arches Drive-In and ordered a double burger basket and coffee from the poof-haired blond wearing sprayed-on white Capri pants, low-cut blue blouse, and a tiny white yachting cap. No visible panty line, Steve noted with interest, as she sashayed away with his order. He got out of the truck and called the number in the Velzy ad from the drive-in's pay phone. No answer.

After scarfing the burger and loading up on caffeine, the surfer on sabbatical left an oversize tip for the enticing blond and drove to the Newport Beach library.

The crisscross directory had a street address for the telephone number but no name was listed. He found the street on the library's city map and made tracks for the location near the beach.

It was 10:45 AM and the summer day promised to be another scorcher with a slight offshore breeze. The detective pulled up across the street of a faded-green, stucco Balboa peninsula duplex. It was only a couple miles away from Estep's pad. Odds were that the dumpy two-story building was a rental since it had a wearied, neglected look.

He knocked hard twice on the solid-oak front door. Nobody home, apparently, or nobody answering, so Lund had no choice but to wait it out, sitting in the truck, until the resident showed.

Finally, after Steve had spent two hours roasting in the summer heat while reading his dog-eared *Moby Dick* paperback, a skinny, long-haired youngster in khaki shorts and straw lifeguard lid walked up to the duplex and entered the house. Steve hopped out of his simmering hot truck, locked it, and then rapped on the front door.

"Whatcha want, dude?" asked longhair as he opened the door halfway, a beer can clutched in his grasp.

"Came to check out the Velzy you have for sale. Can I see it? I couldn't reach you by phone," explained Steve.

"You're too late. Sold it yesterday. Sorry." The young stud started to close the door.

"Wait a second!" barked Steve as he put his hand against the closing door. "When did you buy it from Velzy's shop?"

"When did I buy it? What the fuck difference does it make to you? The board is sold. Gone. Understand?" the skinny guy angrily shouted in Steve's face.

"Listen, buddy. I'm tracking down a stolen Velzy surfboard for a friend. Just give me your name and I'll check with Dale Velzy to verify you bought it from him, or tell me where you got it. No need for me to contact the Newport Beach Police, in that case, about a possible stolen board," bluffed Steve.

"Name's Ralph Baker. Now fuck off!" he answered huffily and slammed the door hard.

"Thanks for all your fucking help, Ralphie!" yelled Steve at the closed door. He spun around and stomped back to his panel truck, slamming the door as he got in. Guess that's the end of that hot lead, he growled to himself as he jammed the stick shift into low and popped the clutch. The petulant rustbucket lurched down the street.

Back at Estep's empty place, Steve opened his first cold beer of the day and called Velzy's shop, where Hap confirmed that, indeed, the board purchase by "Ralphie" Baker was valid.

Kenny had left a note that he would be on the beach or surfing near the Newport Pier after his one o'clock class at the JC, skipping zoology lab. Lucky day for Francis Frog, destined to be sacrificed on a marble slab for science at one-fifteen that afternoon.

Steve, lugging his big stick under one arm and a cold six-pack in the other hand, met Kenny and two of his roomies next to the nearby pier. It was a low tide, suck-out session with mushburger waves. Mostly groms were out on the dinky two-footers, milking the surge for all it was worth. No good for the big Peterson.

"What are you doing down here, anyway?" Steve bitched at Kenny. "You can't be that desperate for a shitty little ride."

"I'm trying to ditch a certain young lady who's vacation-ing here this week from Minnesota. Sonja knows where I live, of course, since she's been spending *mucho* sack time there," grinned Estep. "But now she's been exhibiting a sudden jealous streak and also whispered in my ear about extending her vacation. Her love boat has hit the reef. I don't need the hassle and whining."

"Say, Ken, I'm headed to San Diego country tomorrow morning. I'm going to call Mr. Hess and let him know the

Velzy ad was legit and then I'm journeying south. What about your doper friend in Carlsbad? Do you think he would be worth looking up about my Gloria search?"

"You mean Bennie Benny. He's stoked on surfing these days. Hangin' at the beach, living in his pickup camper and baked on meth most of the time. Benny drives a bootleg taxi at Del Mar during the horseracing season. You can give it a try at Carlsbad. Old red '40 Ford pickup with a redwood camper on it, can't miss it."

"Thanks for the tip," said Steve.

"We've been nabbing good morning surf at the Bluffs and down Dana Point way up until now," continued Kenny. "D Point has been firing nifty rockets. Wanna go south in the AM? Surf is supposed to pick up again tomorrow."

"Yeah. We can zip down to Dana tomorrow. I have to stop there anyway and leave some fliers with the other boarders. I'll take my truck—you can take your own heap. I want to swing into Laguna Main and Salt Creek to drop fliers there too. We can meet at Doheny Beach Park and rip up Dana all morning. Hope your surf prediction isn't bogus. Let's polish off these brews before they get warm. Two apiece, my friends, so drink up!"

The next morning Steve found motoring through downtown Laguna Beach was a breeze at 9:00. No tourist and beachgoer traffic at that hour. The gray-bearded Laguna Greeter was standing at his usual sidewalk post just outside Hotel Laguna. Steve gave him a long honk and a rooftop wave, which lit up the old geezer's face as he waved back.

Laguna's coastline is notched with a myriad of rocky coves and sandy pocket beaches with summerhouses glued to the ice plant-covered cliffs. Some of the beaches have great bodysurfing beach breaks, but that part of the California coast has zip offshore waves for boarders, the exception being the north side of Laguna's Main Beach in winter and Salt Creek at the southern perimeter of town. Salt Creek could be a hot breaking spot over its sandbar when a Baja storm kicked up a running south swell. Downtown Main was flat so Steve left fliers with the local surfers hanging out there playing two-man volleyball.

Main Beach was the volleyball Mecca of Orange County, and the six sand courts were dominated from late morning to dusk by a loosely organized bunch of college and social dropouts who played V-ball there every day, year around. A cult similar to surfers but more territorial, localized, and didn't migrate much to other beach venues.

Salt Creek, at the southern end of Laguna, is a lengthy stretch of white sand and has a close-in surf break. Steve stopped to chat up two peroxide blonds who didn't surf but surely were nice to look at on both sides. All oiled up and basting ninety-five percent of their tender pink bodies. Steve jotted down their phone numbers for future use and papered the parked surfer cars. He spent an hour on the Peterson showing off his stuff to the pink ladies—staying out of the locals' way and their waves.

When he reached Doheny Beach a little after 10:30, Kenny's beater Plymouth woodie was empty, so he unloaded the Peterson and paddled out to the Dana Point lineup. A hazy blue glare melded the sky and sea into a blur at the horizon. The indistinct sets coming in were irregular but makeable three-footers, not the predicted fours.

Estep was straddling his nine-ten stick waiting for his big wave of the day to show. "Nothin' much out here. Wanna go to 'Nofre and see what's brewing?" Kenny suggested.

"Might as well. Your tsunami ain't coming today and it only takes a few minutes to buzz down there," agreed Steve as they turned boards shoreward. The bounty hunter papered the cars in the parking lot with Gloria fliers before leaving Doheny.

San Onofre is the premier surfing spot of California when the swell is humping and cranking out five-footers. With its head-high peaks, a smooth summer glide can be had before the afternoon onshore chop sets in. Kenny and

Steve spent part of the day playing "chicken" on each other's wave. One would catch the break, the other would cut and block, right in front. "I'm gonna give you a skeg slice for your other shoulder!" threatened Estep as he was cut off his wave again by Steve.

"Ya gotta retaliate with more aggression, like a local would," retorted Lund as he slipped past Kenny on a bottom section.

About three-thirty, Steve decided to drive on to the north San Diego surfing beaches. "I'm going to Dago for a few days and give it a look-see, check out the summer surf, and sniff around for Gloria. Be back, so see ya when I see ya," he yelled to Kenny and stroked easily into a three-foot roller for a long lazy ride to the beach. He tacked a Gloria flier on the pole of the thatched beach *palapa* and passed some out to the regulars lounging in the palm frond shade.

Steve headed south from 'Nofre listening to an episode of "Johnny Dollar" on the surf wagon's AM radio. The exploits of the "insurance investigator with the action-packed expense account" kept him interested until the hills turned the signal to static.

It would take two or three days to canvass the ten scruffy beach towns lining the thirty-five-mile stretch of coastline from Carlsbad and south to the Mexican border. The exception to scruffy towns would be upscale La Jolla where Gloria probably wasn't.

San Clemente, a pseudo-Spanish funky village with low-key surf shops, Mexican *mercados*, and fading pastel paint jobs, Twenties-built vacation bungalows near the beach was his next stop. As many surfers that could be tolerated by an absentee or laid-back landlords inhabited most of the stucco residences. Most of the garages were surfer-inhabited cheapo sub-rentals. San Clemente had some surf but the main attraction for living there was its close proximity to San Onofre. Steve papered the village with fliers and downed three tacos plus two Coronas at a downtown *mercado.*

There are zero towns between San Onofre and the jarhead city of Oceanside. Since there was no public access along the twenty miles of Camp Pendleton's USMC beachfront, Steve drove straight to the Carlsbad turnoff and stopped there on the highway to check the surf. Didn't spot surfer one, as the Pacific was pacific with a slight chop. He next pulled in at South Carlsbad Beach and schmoozed with a trio of draft-age Escondido boarders. They weren't going back out to surf two-footers but were not eager to head back to their inland, sweltering-hot, avocado farm homes. He left some fliers and dropped three baggies on them for keeping their eyes open.

Steve drove slowly into sleepy Leucadia, which was taking a summer late-afternoon siesta. No point in traveling any farther south since no surf and no surfers around. He checked in early at the Moonlight Beach Motel, a sandy place in and out, featuring a sky-blue stucco exterior and the typical red clay tile roof. After buying a giant burrito at the adjoining Mexican café, he walked the long block to the beach. Sipping on a cold beer, with a backup brew in the burrito sack, he watched the hot summer sun extinguish itself in the ocean out beyond San Clemente Island.

Walking back toward his motel, the detective found a locals' beer bar with a pool table in the rear and proceeded to lose six very close straight games of deadly eight-ball to a pair of young Leucadia pool sharks. At five bucks a game it was thirty bucks, plus a quartet of draft beers, all down the toilet. Steve didn't take the two hustlers up on their "get even—double or nothing" offer. That night he slept like a rock in the sandy sheets of the Moonlight Beach Motel—not rated by AAA nor by anyone else.

In the morning Steve hit the donut shop for a sack of cinnamon rolls, plus a large container of coffee, and walked down the street to Grandview Beach.

"Seen Benny around?" the bounty hunter inquired of the lanky bronzed surfer with the hawk-like nose who sat on the beach filing nicks out of the skeg on his board. Steve handed him a warm roll from the sack.

"Ya mean Bennie Benny?" the local replied with a wicked grin, taking a half-moon munch out of the roll.

"Yeah, that's the guy. He's a friend of a friend."

"You can usually find him a little ways down from here at Stonesteps, or Swami's, just south of Encinitas. He hangs out at those beaches. Don't buy at his first price, if you get my drift."

"I know where those spots are and thanks for the tip," said Steve as he dropped a newspaper of leaf on the waterman's overturned board. Steve handed his informant a few Gloria fliers and said to look sharp—a grand may come his way.

"Anytime, for a little good weed, my friend," replied the hawk-nosed browned surfer with a Cheshire cat grin.

There were a few teenage kids hanging at Stonesteps and no Bennie mobile in sight, so he drove on down old 101 the few miles to Encinitas and Swami's. The golden, onion-shaped dome at Swami's always looked out of place in the funky California-styled seaside village. Founded in the late 1930s by Paramahansa Yogananda, who wrote his *Autobiography of a Yogi* there, the Self-Realization Fellowship's hermitage offered yoga and meditation to orange-robed disciples and seekers. But Steve didn't come for yoga.

At Swami's beach in the wintertime, heavy swells rise out of the deep water and jack up on the bar at two hundred yards offshore. The wave drops precipitously at the peak and has a long, fast shoulder to the right. Island-style, winter storm double overheads—perfect for boarders.

A few overnighters were parked on the shore-side edge of the highway at the north end of Del Mar's beach. The ratty, red Ford pickup, burdened by a bleached-out redwood camper, resembled a Romany gypsy's caravan. Steve pulled up behind Benny's rig. There was no sign of life so he got out and banged on the camper's door, yelling, "Bennie Benny!"

"Who the hell is it?" came a muffled reply from inside, after a second hard bang on the door.

"It's Steve Lund. A friend of Kenny Estep's," yelled his visitor at the closed-up camper truck.

"Don't wet your pants. I'll be out in a sec," came a mumbled response.

The camper's door squeaked open and a reefer haze rolled out of the door like the smoke from a smoldering campfire. A short, stocky guy about twenty-five, red hair matching the truck and clad in olive-green Army skivvies, eased himself outside.

Benny shook Steve's offered hand grudgingly, apparently to show—like the old French custom—he was not going to run his visitor through with a rapier. Benny's tense body language said he would just as soon run a stranger through as shake the offered hand.

"What's up? Kenny need some Dex? You wanna buy some uppers?" inquired the testy pill merchant, whose red facial stubble matched that on his head.

"No. Not looking to make a buy. I brought you some Acapulco Gold, though, primo stuff, so you know I'm not a Narc. Just searching for a particular missing girl. Have you seen the gal on this flier, or her stick and wheels, down this way in the past few weeks? She could be hanging out between Carlsbad and Pacific Beach. If your eagle eye spots her, it's worth a thousand big ones. Here are some fliers to spread around."

"The price is right—I could use a thousand smackers. Yeah, that's for sure," said Benny. "I'll pass your fliers around and call you if any results. Sure you don't need a bag of zoom for yourself?"

"Thanks, but I'll pass on the jelly beans for now. Surf been up down this way lately?"

"Look right out there, my friend. Decent enough bumps in the ocean for ya?"

Steve turned and now noticed a series of swells coming in, humping up about two hundred plus yards out. "Guess I'll paddle out and snag a few before they fade out. Coming, Benny?"

"Yeah, later. Don't wait for me. Have to have a little morning boost first," said the grizzled pill dispenser as he crawled back into his cubbyhole.

Steve took the big Peterson off the rack, trotted down to the beach, and stroked quickly out beyond the break line. The morning swell was not as strong as he would have liked it, but the waterman eased into a three-footer and gave it a long ride south. Riding the edge of the lip, he dropped down into the blue-green core and carved a tight bottom turn, then skimmed along in the hollow fading tube, finally edging back up onto the lip as the swell faded out. After an hour of ocean communion, guilt set in. Steve rode a final wave to shore and loaded the Log back onto his truck.

Steve had already pulled a tube of pot from the surf truck's rack for Bennie. He stopped now at Bennie's camper truck to deliver it, knocking hard on the camper's door. "Here's that sample hit for you as promised. I'll bring some more to you on my way back from San Diego," he told the doper, handing him the "News" as Bennie stepped out.

An unmarked white Ford sedan quickly rolled up and skidded to a stop next to Bennie's truck. A pair of dark-suited, butch-haired, heavyweight Anglos suddenly eased themselves out of their police-special sedan. Both suits simultaneously drew blued snub-nosed .38 automatics from shoulder holsters. Plainclothes, but obviously narcs, handcuffs dangled at the ready from their left hands as the pair exchanged grins of self-satisfaction.

"Caught ourselves a surf rat making his dope delivery house call, Mr. O'Riley," said the first cop, as he plucked the rolled-up newspaper sheet from a shocked Bennie's hand with his fingertips.

"Correct, Mr. Kolowski," said his partner, a heavy-set Irishman, who sported an ex-boxer's flattened nose and mashed-flat ears. He had cool, disdainful dark eyes and a special look of nastiness about him.

"You're both under arrest, dopers. Drug-dealing felonies for starters. That's for sure. We'll give ya the long list of multiple felony charges at the station," growled Kolowski, as he poked his nose into the newspaper tube, then slipped it into a plastic evidence bag.

"Down on your knees, the both of you. Hands behind your back. Don't move a fuckin' inch from that position until we say so. It don't take much to piss us off and make us think you're resisting arrest. Right, Mr. Kolowski?" said the Mick cop.

"Correct, again, Mr. O'Riley," said the grinning Polish cop.

The two narcotics officers efficiently snapped the steel handcuffs tightly on the wrists of the two surfers kneeling in the parking lot gravel.

"We're hauling you two dopers in for booking, and your vehicles are gonna be towed in for a drug search," said Officer O'Riley.

"You two officers of the law didn't witness anything very illegal here. Certainly no felonies committed. The two of you might think so right now. No point discussing points of law here while we're cuffed and on our knees. Are you guys sure this haul-in is necessary? What if we both just leave your city now?" said Steve.

"Yea, we're damned sure, surfer boy," retorted O'Riley. "Think you're pretty fucking smart, talking jailhouse law. A real wiseass fucking courthouse legal eagle is what we have here, Mr. Kolowski. You think the law is in your law books? It isn't. *We* are the law here. Got that, doper? We love your kind here in Del Mar. I suppose you want me and Mr. Kolowski here to believe that oregano or tea leaves are in that tube of newspaper your buddy here was holding as we drove up. Maybe you're just a newspaper delivery boy, right? Fat fuckin' chance of that. We all know this was a felony drug deal, plain and simple."

"When our boys at the station strip-search your panel truck, they'll find your stash," snarled Kolowski. "I'm positive of that. Then we'll nail your ass for felony possession, dealing, and transporting of drugs for sale. Count on ten years in state prison, hard time. That's a fact, delivery boy. Those heavies in Folsom will just love your sweet white ass."

The Polish cop held the muzzle of his steel blue .38 at Steve's temple, then delivered a hard soccer-style kick into the kneeling surfer's ribcage with his heavy police brogan. Steve grunted at the sharp pain as he fell hard onto his left side in the gravel.

"Get back on your knees, doper. That didn't hurt ya, it's just the first shot across the bow," warned Kolowski.

Steve struggled to regain his kneeling position, breathing heavily. He glanced over at the wide-eyed and scared-shitless Bennie, who was watching the live action from six feet away. The Irish copper hadn't made a move on Bennie, yet. Maybe this was the beginning of the classic good cop-bad cop routine, thought Steve.

"Let's get these potheads in the car, Mr. O'Riley. You two dickheads get your asses up and walk slowly over to the Ford. No quick moves, and no talking in the car, unnerstand? You do not want us to stop the car on the way to the station, unnerstand? We don't want to explain any injuries you two dopers got while resisting arrest, unnerstand?" instructed Kolowski.

Bennie and Steve staggered to their feet, shuffled slowly over to the police sedan, and stopped next to the rear door, saying nothing to each other. They were roughly shoved into the backseat and handcuffed to a steel bar running the length of the seat behind them. Bennie looked scared and was shaking—ready to say anything to save his sorry ass from hard time in Folsom Prison.

Lund kicked Bennie in the leg and slowly mouthed the words "Not Guilty and No Felony," receiving a slight nod of agreement. Bennie Benny is gonna be my weak link in this bust, thought Steve. I just hope he keeps it zipped.

After arriving inside the barbed-wire-topped parking area at the rear of the Del Mar Police Station, the handcuffed drug-dealing suspects were unlocked from the restraining bar and yanked out of the sedan by the good guy-bad guy officers of the law.

The DMPD station, located a few miles inland, was a two-story, unpainted, concrete-block cop container, budget built and dreary looking. Its roof bristled with police radio antennas. The windows were all barred and the door to the rear entrance was solid gray steel with a double dead-bolt lock. No door handle and no apparent way to escape out the door.

"They won't find any weed in my truck," whispered Steve to Bennie as they were perp-walked inside the station, a cop close, front and rear. "Just cool it. Don't let them rat you out."

"Shut up!" yelled Kolowski, behind Steve, as he slapped his open left hand alongside Steve's head, knocking the arrestee up against the concrete hallway wall.

"Remember, Officer K," said Steve, "I can't answer your questions during any interrogations if I can't hear what the fuck you are asking me."

"You still got one good ear for now, doper boy, so keep your smartass yap shut tight until I ask you sumpin. Got that?"

Steve nodded once. There's not going to be any quick and easy way out of this bust, he thought. Damn good thing I don't have a conviction record for anything other than a couple of traffic tickets. These thugs won't find any rap sheet, priors, or an ounce of grass on me. Nothin' inside my truck—not a speck of weed—unless these low-life narcs plant something there themselves. Hope Bennie is as clean.

Bennie and Steve were booked on five felony counts each, strip-searched, fingerprinted, and photographed for mug shots. A request at booking to make one phone call was denied, no reason given, and Steve's second request when the processing was over was ignored. The two were led away to separate small, cell-like rooms at the rear of the station. A scratched-up steel-gray office table and two matching straight-back chairs were the only items in the stark and unadorned interrogation room. A head-high, barred and grimy window was centered on one lime-green block wall. The overhead egg-crated fluorescent light tubes were on the fritz, giving the green room a shimmering, epileptic glow and unnatural aura. The yellowed plastic fixture box made noises as if it were electrocuting a swarm of captive insects buzzing around inside.

From the corridor, Steve could be viewed through the one-way slot window set eye-level in the steel door. The iron ring cemented into the floor in the center of the room was used when the perp fastened there was considered "unruly and uncooperative." Getting fastened securely there in leg chains while cuffed alone for hours will cool down and loosen up ninety-nine percent of the Gray Bar Del Mar Hotel's belligerent guests. The other one percent didn't give a fuck about cooperation and didn't.

Steve wasn't subjected to leg chains and the iron ring treatment; arms tightly cuffed behind his back to the cold steel chair was thought by the two dicks to be sufficient punishment, so far, for his continued obstinateness. Steve sat motionless on the cold steel chair.

He must have been sitting still for over two hours, getting chilled and stiff, wearing only his cutoffs and a short sleeved sweatshirt. His ribcage hurt where the cop had kicked it. The pale-green, grimy asphalt tile floor was cold on his bare feet so he kept them resting back on the heels.

Finally, the heavy steel door clanked open and Officer Kolowski sauntered in, sipping coffee from a large Styrofoam cup. "We're going to have a little private chat, you and me. Make it easy on yourself. Maybe we can cut a deal, you and me. Just tell us where your fucking stash of weed is in your truck. Save us a lot of time and effort. Maybe I can get some of the felony charges reduced or dropped. You could cut that ten years of state prison hard time to only a couple of easy ones in our nice, comfy county jail. If you talk now, you'll lighten your load considerably. Why make it tough on yourself for no good reason? We know, and you know, you're guilty as sin," wheedled the Polish cop. "Whaddaya say, Lund?"

"Sorry, Officer K, just can't help you out. Wasn't hauling any load of grass, or peddling it either. Just happened to be delivering one small birthday gift to a friend, from another friend, when you two happened to drive by. Certainly not a felony at less than an ounce, you know that. Just doing a 'Happy Birthday Bennie' deed. As a favor."

"You're a lying son of a bitch!" yelled hot-tempered Kolowski, as he slapped Steve hard across the jaw and left ear, knocking the chair and Steve onto the tiled concrete floor. The furious cop reached down, grabbed a fistful of sweatshirt and jerked his suspect back upright on the chair.

Steve just looked at him and calmly said, "I have to piss. I've been sitting here for hours." His ear was ringing and his head was beginning to throb.

"Just piss where you're sittin' and stew in your own juice. You're not going anywhere—not even to the john—'til I get some answers out of you. Where is that fucking dope you're peddling? Where did you stash it? Do ya want us to finish ripping the guts out of your panel truck? We'll rip every fucking thing out of it and turn it upside down if that's what you want."

Steve didn't answer, just sat staring straight ahead.

"OK. Play this your way, fine. Stew in your own piss and shit right there. We're in no big hurry. But why not make it easy for yourself and your chum? Give up the dope and we'll get the DA to go light on both you and your buddy," promised the smiling Polish narc in his smarmy, used-car salesman voice.

"Your five-count felony case against us consists of you two narcs supposedly observing a delivery of drugs for sale. Wrong. A possible transfer of a very small amount of grass between friends. A gift. Less than an ounce and no money exchanged hands, right? There was not even a blade or sniff of weed on me or in my truck, right? No prints of mine on anything. Right? So what criminal acts do you have to prosecute, Officer? I'll tell you. A possible misdemeanor violation, at best, against a first offender. It will take you two some outstanding testifying, or lying, to convince a judge or jury to convict Bennie and me on the flimsy and scanty evidence you two officers of the law possess. Your so-called felony bust won't hold up in court. None of it will. A sharp legal eagle can even make Keystone Cop comedy fools of you and your Irish partner. Want that to happen on your hometown turf? I think not. Want the press involved? I think not. Why not turn us loose with our promise that your fair city will never, ever, see either one of us again? I mean never. Isn't that better than a possible misdemeanor conviction for you and your partner? You're not getting a cash bounty and you're not paid by the conviction. I know that. Go talk it over with your buddy O'Riley and your DA. See if they don't both agree. I'm certainly not confessing to any felony drug charges of packing, hauling, or selling any drugs and neither will Bennie."

"You're so fuckin' smart, aren't ya, Mr. Drug Dealer. You and your fuckin' legal eagle talk," snarled the enraged Kolowski as he again slapped Steve hard on the right side of the head. The chair and Steve both rocked sideways but didn't tip all the way over this time.

"You can beat the shit out of me, Kolowski, and your hyenas can rip the guts out of my truck, but it won't do you any fucking good. There's nothing there. Those are the facts, Officer K."

One of his favorite interrogation techniques, thought Steve. No cuts or broken bones, just some facial bruises from "resisting arrest" or "falling down."

"I'm telling you again, Officer K, I gotta piss, starting right now!" shouted Steve.

Officer O'Riley happened to walk into the room just as steamy yellow liquid started dripping off the edge of Steve's chair. It began to form a small yellow pool on the green tile floor. O'Riley stared at their prisoner.

"Now look at that! Kid pissed in his knickers. Shall we make him lick it up, or just let him stew in his own juice?" laughed Kolowski.

"Just let him stew in it awhile. Let's go out and talk," said the Irishman, not smiling.

Kolowski casually walked over and poured his remaining warm coffee into Steve's lap without a word. Both cops turned and walked out of the room, locking the steel door behind them.

Steve smiled grimly to himself while calmly sitting in the steaming warm mix of coffee and urine. Another hour passed, probably longer. He heard occasional police sirens leaving and steel doors slamming shut.

It was chilly and damp in the greenish-blue light of the interrogation room. The overhead light fixture kept up its intermittent flickering and artificial bug-buzzing sound. He sat quietly and zoned out about his fate while his gut was growling for food.

Officer O'Riley came back into the piss-smelling room, alone and still unsmiling. He walked behind Steve and unlocked the steel cuffs that shackled his arrestee to the wet chair, careful not to step in anything nasty. Steve began to slowly move his stiff arms and shoulders around to regain some feeling in them.

"Get up!" said O'Riley. "We're going to turn you two druggies loose. Not what I would do. The DA said he didn't want to fuck around trying a crummy misdemeanor pot case. He said to tell you two dickheads that thirty minutes is all the time you two have left in the city of Del Mar. Don't ever come back, even to just play the ponies or hit the surf.

"If Kolowski or I ever see you druggies on our turf again, your arrest and felony conviction for drugs will be a guaranteed certainty. We will find a stash of pot next time and you very likely will also be found guilty of resisting arrest. You do understand me, don't you, Mr. Steven Lund?"

"Yeah. I understand and so will Bennie. Don't worry. We'll stay off your turf and crummy beach. Did your hyenas leave my truck in running condition and my stuff in it?"

"It'll get you out of our city on time, Lund. The interior received a strip and toss job, nothing major; in fact, it's probably an improvement," said the Irish cop with another fake grin. He walked Steve out to the parking lot after signing him out at the station desk and handing over the truck keys and Steve's wallet. Bennie was already out in the parking lot, standing beside his camper truck with a grin on his face. He looked a little frazzled and pale.

"Did they rough you up, Lund? That Polack is one nasty son of a bitch. He knows how to bang you around without leaving any marks or cuts. I didn't let him knock anything out of me. I did like you said, play dumb, say'n nuthin'."

"Yeah," said Steve. "He belted me around some until he made sure I heard church bells ringing. I told you they could get rough, but not to squawk and we would walk," Steve said, as he opened the door to his surf wagon and perused the damage.

"Kolowski and O'Riley didn't have much of a case. They came up empty searching me and my truck. It's time for both of us to haul ass out of this shitty beach burg. Surf isn't that great here anyway, so no great loss. You can set up shop a little farther north or south of here. Be careful, Bennie. See you around."

"Yeah. See ya, Lund. By the way, where the hell did you stash your grass? I know you're packin' a load of leaf. See my paddleboard racked up next to my board on top of the camper? It's hollow, with a cork in the ass end to drain out the water. It doesn't go into the water because that's my pharmacy stash," admitted Bennie.

"You don't need to know where mine is," replied Steve as he climbed into his trashed panel truck and started the engine. Both front seat cushions of the old Ford had been sliced open like hamburger buns. The interior paneling and headliner were gone. All his clothes and the rest of his gear were tossed into a big jumble at the back. Steve had not even looked up at the surf rack, still stuffed tight with Acapulco Gold. The rack still held the untouched Peterson. Good thing the narcs couldn't smell worth a damn with that load of weed right under their noses, thought Steve, as he slowly pulled out of the DMPD yard and waved a thumb up to Bennie exiting right behind him. He sighed with relief at his narrow escape from Folsom.

Nearly A. Felon backtracked a few miles up the coast from Del Mar to funky Encinitas, a coastal village inhabited mainly by gnarly, bump-kneed surfers. The broad and flat beach had decent year-around waves, warm water, and a plethora of budget-priced motels—plenty of cheap taco stands, burger joints, and beer bars too. A good place to rest up and reload for a day or so before resuming the ongoing Gloria quest.

After checking into the Sea View Motel, a U-shaped, pastel pink-colored, concrete block establishment on a side street—near the beach but with no view of anything other than a parking lot—Steve showered, dressed, and unloaded everything out of the Ford and onto the bed and floor in his motel room.

Gray duct tape did the job of patching the cut-up seats of the truck, taping down the flooring in the rear, and sealing the mattress pad that had been sliced open like a loaf of bread by the Del Mar PD assholes. After reassembling all his camping gear, clothes, and food, he repacked everything into the panel truck.

It was now early afternoon and Steve was starving. He moseyed a few blocks up to the main drag in the warm sun and into Manuel's Taqueria where he ordered *huevos rancheros* with beans, *carne asada*, and a dozen tortillas. Two ice-cold Dos Equis washed down the heaping plate of Cali-Mex grub and helped cool off the chili-laced salsa fire on his tongue and in his belly while three aspirins helped mask the surfer's sore and swollen jaw from last night's interrogation by the semi-tough narc cop.

Afterwards, Steve walked off the truckload of Mexican fare, checking out the surf down the street-end from the "luxurious" Sea View Motel. Waves were flat with a low-tide suckout in effect. Surfboards, jammed into the sand nose first, resembled oversized peeled bananas scattered haphazardly on the white sand beach.

Back at the motel he called Bettie from the pay phone outside his room to see what was up. "*Nada.* Nuttin' new for ya, Dick Tracy. Bristow hasn't killed himself either. Not yet, anyway," replied Bettie.

"Glad all is well at Fort Bettie. I'll check back in with you in a few days. *Ciao,*" said Steve.

The next morning Steve woke up at seven with his head aching, courtesy of the Del Mar dicks. He walked down the street to a small, yellow-stuccoed café for pancakes and coffee. "It's hard to screw up pancakes, but you came close," he told the slow-moving, cud-chewing, bleached-blond waitress, as he swallowed a couple of aspirins with his lukewarm coffee. Pseudo-blondie just gave him a deaf and dumb look and led away.

Steve packed up his truck and headed south the short way to upscale La Jolla. Taking a San Diego County road inland from Solana Beach, Steve bypassed off-limits Del Mar, then cut back to the beach on Torrey Pines Road to La Jolla. There should be some fine waves to be had at Windansea.

At the north end of La Jolla, the sandbars on both sides of Scripps Pier turn out reliable peaks year-around. Not great, but consistent threes on the incoming tides. San Diego State College students and staff head there from their campus on the eastern edge of downtown San Diego to catch a few waves before or after classes. It was pointless to blanket the inland campus with fliers, so he concentrated on the beach crowd and close-by parking on the bluff.

Salubrious. Now that was the exact word for La Jolla. Picture-postcard ocean vistas, warm weather and water, plus scenic orange and pink sunsets over the Pacific. No real seasons there—seldom too hot or windy, never too cold. Not much challenging surf though, except from time to time at Windansea and Horseshoe Reef to the north.

The out-of-towner parked on a dead-end street near Windansea Beach for a quick wave check and decided to get in an hour of surfing. The mid-morning sets were cresting three to four feet and just over a hundred yards out. Good-looking sets and only a half-dozen boarders out to jockey with on a wave. He trudged across the locals' Pumphouse turf and waxed up near the kelp-laced frieze at the shoreline. Narrowed, hooded eyes stared in his direction from the beach seawall. Screw them, he thought.

At Windansea, the adolescent cultish crowd of local bucks thought they "owned" the beach and the break in front of them. LOCALS ONLY was charcoaled on the sea-wall. An outsider would have to show his canines, not get bluffed, and be board proficient to grab his share of rides. No way could a female outsider surf there. No way. Gloria would not be here.

Steve paddled the Peterson out to the point and set up. Three local hotshots came hustling out a few minutes later. Turf-war time. One pair moved in close and set up outside on his left. A third one sat bobbing on his board on his immediate right. Trouble brewing.

When he dropped into the first wave of a set, the three young locals just sat pat. Steve stroked back into his spot and then made his move to catch a second wave. The guy on the right suddenly shot his board right into the path of the Peterson. Steve quickly flipped out of the wave and back over the crest. "What the fuck are you doing, Bozo?" he yelled at the heavy-set punk. Windansea dude stared hard but did not acknowledge the challenge.

The two boarders to his left took turns taking every wave early and then popping up and out, blocking Steve at every chance. As the four surfers jockeyed for position on each set of waves, a game of "chicken" developed. The visiting waterman wasn't to be shut down or scared off. A local was shoved off his board with a Lund straight-arm. Steve crashed hard into another. When both combatants hit the water, they scrambled for boards, saving their sticks from being washed into shore.

As he dropped in on Steve, the kid on the right had his board plowed under by the Peterson, like a destroyer downing a whaleboat. After an hour of joisting with the Windansea bunch, the visiting surfer thought he had made his point and presence known and caught a heavy right shoulder back to shore.

The heavyset Bozo crowed loudly when he came in a minute later and dried off. "That'll show him whose beach and break this is! Fuck off, outsider!" He directed another malevolent stare at the unwelcome waterman.

Steve walked back to his truck with his board and racked it up. He grabbed an oil stick rag, dunked it into his spare gas can and put it into a plastic bag. Grabbing a taped five-dollar roll of quarters and a couple of kitchen matches, he strolled back to the beach where the rowdy locals were sitting on the Pumphouse seawall, girl watching. They gave Steve the stink eye when he showed up again on their turf.

Grinning, the visiting boarder walked over to Bozo's beach towel lying on the beach near the wall and dropped the gas-soaked rag on it. Steve casually struck a match on the concrete seawall and flipped it onto the oil rag. It instantly blossomed a smoky orange and black. As the towel started to burn, Bozo jumped off the seawall and rushed the waiting arsonist. "You son of a bitch!" the local loudmouth shouted. The four teen girls hanging with the La Jolla bunch screamed and dashed up the Pumphouse steps.

Steve nearly dodged the swinging punch launched by the charging young bull, but a fist smashed hard into his right shoulder, spinning the visitor down on the sand and to his knees.

Grabbing a handful of beach sand and scrambling quickly up as Bozo rushed in again, Steve threw the sand squarely into the eyes of his attacker. His right fist clutching the tube of quarters, he sledgehammered the tube of rolled silver deep into his opponent's gut. The big lummox folded and dropped to the beach, blinded and gasping for air.

"Don't get up or you'll get more of the same," snarled Steve, while eyeing the rest of the unruly pack. Two other buddies started to make a move on him but stopped short when their intended target threatened, "Stay where you are; I'm going to leave now, so don't make me come back here and make a bonfire out of your boards."

The pair backed down, yapping like pups for Steve to "Get the fuck outta here, you crazy bastard!" The unwelcome surfer gave them the finger, brazenly turned his back on the cowed beach hounds, and strolled back to his truck. Guess I won't bother asking them for help finding Gloria, he said to himself while massaging his bruised shoulder.

Steve drove south to Pacific Beach (PB to locals), party capital of all San Diego beaches and the logical place to search for Gloria while perusing the oceanfront party house scene along the boardwalk from there to Mission Beach. PB is where both action and good surfing is found. Just bring beer and grass and you're welcome, day or night, to hang. And this is where I would hang out, if I were her, reasoned Steve.

At Ocean Beach (OB), to the south of Mission Beach (Mission), the peaks hump up outside the San Diego River mouth. OB was therefore a prime surfing spot, and famous for the time when Duke Kahanamoku gave surfing exhibitions on his huge redwood surfboard during the summer of 1916. Today, the local, hard-ass surfing crowd knows swimmers at OB as "speed bumps." Steve set out to post and distribute fliers all along the long sandy beaches from PB to OB.

He checked out the pearl string of south county beach cafes, including Nati's, a popular morning café and surfer hangout. No sign or leads on his elusive quarry.

The Ocean Beach Pier Café served the best coffee and donuts on the coast, so it was another must visit morning place. Pacific Shores, the local's number one beer bar, had eighteen taps pouring drafts, and Steve managed to sample their entire selection of draft beer during his three-day San Diego sojourn.

Sunny days, warm ocean and hot ladies—a perfect threesome for a quick summer venture. The days and nights of nonstop searching and partying had concluded on two occasions with "overnighters" in his truck, with blue-eyed and petite Susan from Phoenix and rough and ready Loretta from Laredo. The big-boned and breasted brunette, a Texas tornado, taught him some reverse cowgirl bronco-busting moves that left him stiff and sore the next day.

Sunset Cliffs (Cliffs), to the south, was showing off the best summer surf of the San Diego area so far. Surfers there told him the big winter and spring Baja hurricane storms could crank up eight- to ten-foot heavy peaks for a week. "Call me collect when one comes and I'll be right down," said Steve.

The rough dirt foot trail to Sunset was a slippery bitch down the eroded sandstone cliffs while toting a big board overhead. One false step, and it's Ding City or worse for your board as it flip-flops down to the beach. Watching tenderfoot surfers navigate up and down Sunset's cliffs was a spectator sport for the beach crowd, as they waited for the next Charlie Chaplin pratfall show.

North Beach (North) sometimes had decent surf in the summer, they said, but it wasn't now or to be soon. Flat and nobody out. A few tourist types getting some rays on the beach. He didn't bother with fliers.

Imperial Beach (IB or Fecal City) was known for rips to ride out on to the break line—when there was one. Not a brilliant idea to get ocean water in your mouth or ears here, he was warned by other beach dwellers. Fecal City Beach was close to the Tijuana River mouth and its 24/7 flow of shit, and other nasty stuff that was even worse, all rolling into the Pacific Ocean. Steve decided to take a pass on the polluted, tea-colored water at IB. A half-dozen idiots were out in the river break, oblivious and clueless, or perhaps just careless.

He was running low on tubes of grass to deal for info, and San Diego seemed far enough south. Gloria wouldn't be going into Baja, for any reason he could think of anyway, so it was time to head home, restock, and then scour the Santa Monica Bay region more thoroughly, starting in a day or so.

Backtracking to Solana Beach late in the afternoon, Steve checked into the Tide Beach Motel for the night. He wondered if the hundreds of insipid, low-budget motels in Southern California's beach towns were built by the same uninspired, low-bid contractor fond of bland pseudo-Spanish stucco architecture from *Sunset* magazines of the 1920's.

The neon sign of a great Mexican restaurant shimmered alongside on the highway in Solana Beach near his motel, so he proceeded to load up on a *chile relleno* combo plate and a trio of Dos Equis brews. He finished out his San Diego area search with a stroll on the beach to watch the sunset surfers catch the last waves of the day.

When Lund made his routine evening phone call from the motel payphone, Mr. Hess related how a call had come in that afternoon from what sounded like an old drunk who wanted to talk only to Steve Lund, no one else. He professed to have information that was "worth lots of money," said Gloria's father, sounding dubious.

Hess tried in vain to pry a phone number or name from the old guy but finally asked him to call back tomorrow and talk personally to Steve. Steve advised that when the guy called back, if he did, that Hess inform him that Steve would be available to talk business tomorrow evening between five and ten. Hess murmured that he thought a beery phone call from some old rummy during happy hour was not exactly a hot lead, but since it was all they had for now... Promising he'd would be back home the next afternoon, Steve said goodbye, then showered and crashed at the Tide Beach Motel for the night.

It would take a couple hours to travel back to Long Beach, as he planned to stop again to see Kenny in Balboa and Jack Clapp at Dwight's—they might know something new.

The next morning, after a quick pit stop at the donut shop for snails and coffee to go, Steve stopped at Kenny's digs and found the house empty with nary a soul around. No telling where Estep might be mid-morning, so Steve left a note and motored on to Huntington Beach. Jack was open for business but Steve was still full of snails. The hot dog vender had nothing new to tell and hadn't seen Kenny yesterday or today, so the detective drove on to check on Tom at Tin Can Beach.

Old Tom was as full of crap as ever, swearing he'd seen Gloria surfing right near his campsite that week. He couldn't come up with a specific day and hadn't called in with the sighting either, so it evidently wasn't Tom who called Mr. Hess. Steve left him three quarts of suds, plus a baggie, and told the lyin' old fart to keep a sharp eye out; maybe Gloria would show up again.

The Huntington Bluffs still had three to four-footers rolling steadily in with the tide, looking like grandma's tin washboard. There was no rush getting back to Long Beach so might as well surf an hour or so. The waterman leisurely paddled out to catch a fast-closing blue-green tube for a long left, stomping hard on the Peterson's tail to carve a ride-ending spray up and over the fading wave. He stroked back out beyond the breaking rollers again and repeated the process, sometimes rights, then again lefts. He had not lost his touch and timing. The Bluffs were hard to beat for long escalator descents—smooth and steady.

Too soon, it was two and time to hang it up and get back to business. It was conceivable that the anticipated telephone call could be the key to finding the elusive Gloria. There was still some time before meeting Hess, so Steve decided to drive to Downey and review the search with Uncle Bert. The novice detective wanted some tips on how to handle the anonymous phone caller.

They sat down in the back patio as Bert opened a couple of cans of Schlitz.

"Here's the way to do it," the old detective advised. "You're going to set up a meeting with this fellow at a neutral place, in the open and during the daytime. If he really knows where the girl is, promise him some immediate cash, like $200 or $250. The reward is a grand—but you don't want to be packing that kind of cash when you are meeting some stranger. And the reward is for *finding* Gloria, not seeing her somewhere and now she's gone again. Some dope heads I know would lay you out for just the $250, or less."

Steve nodded as his uncle continued. "This guy doesn't have a choice or any other options, since no one else is going to pay a dime for her, correct? Stick to the $200 or $250 cash up-front proposition, at least until you personally verify that it really *is* Gloria, in the flesh. Arrange for the balance payable a day later. A cashier's check is best. If it's not a scam or a mugging, he'll have to agree with your terms. Remember, do the transaction and verification of Gloria yourself, on your own terms, or no deal."

"Sounds like a good plan. I wasn't thinking of a scam or a mugging. I'll handle it myself then, and let you know how it turns out. Thanks, Bert."

Mr. Hess was anxious and fidgety when he met with his young detective. "Maybe I should do the talking myself when the guy calls," he stated emphatically. "After all, I am Gloria's father and it's my money."

"Frankly, I don't think you have the disposition to handle the situation on the phone and then meet with some stranger. If you sound overanxious or threatening, it may queer the deal. Besides, I don't want you to get mugged and perhaps beaten either. It's your reward money, of course. But if I don't handle the call and the transaction, then our deal's off and my search is over, as of right now."

Mr. Hess peered at Steve through his steel-rimmed glasses to determine if he was serious or bluffing. "OK. If that's the way you want it, I guess that is the way it will have to be. Just be sure you don't scare the old guy off or screw it up."

At five-twenty the phone rang and Hess answered. "Yes, he's here. Just a second," he replied and grudgingly handed the telephone over to Steve.

"I know where your girl is," the raspy male voice said.

"You're sure it is Gloria Hess, are you?"

"Damn right I am. She looks just like her picture, though her hair's different. And she's driving a green Chevrolet station wagon. I can show you right where she works. Bring the thousand-dollar reward with you, in cash."

"Where can I meet with you tomorrow and what do you look like? Who are you?"

"Not so fast, Sonny boy. You don't need to know what I look like or who I am right now. We met once but I doubt you'd remember me. Just meet me tomorrow morning, at eleven, on the corner of Venice Boulevard and Pacific Avenue. Do you know where that is? Bring the thou' in twenties."

"I know exactly where that is, and I'll be there tomorrow at eleven sharp. Count on it. I'm driving an old, white Ford panel truck. One thing though, I'm not packing a grand in cash to meet some strange guy on the streets of Venice. I'll have two hundred with me, no more. We can drive to the location where she is to confirm that you have, in fact, located Gloria Hess. If it's her, you'll get the two hundred, in cash, then. I'll have a cashier's check made for the other eight hundred the next day and deliver it to you wherever you want."

"You're trying to screw me out of my reward money!" The agitated caller shouted at Steve. "You'll never show up with the other eight hundred dollars! Why should I trust you to give me the reward money *after* I show you where she is?"

"Listen, old man. That's just how it works. You have my word I will. Anyway, you don't have much choice about the money. It's not like anyone else is going to pay you a dime for her, isn't that right? So it's kind of a take it or leave it situation."

There was a long silence; Steve wondered for a sec if the stranger had hung up without him noticing. Finally, there was a sigh, and he muttered, "I guess you have me by the short hairs, Mr. Lund. I'll see you tomorrow morning at eleven. Don't forget to bring the two C's or the deal is off and I'll talk direct to her daddy. Got that?"

"I have your instructions and you have my word. I'll see you tomorrow then," advised the detective as he hung up the phone.

Lund sat in the sterile living room of the Hess residence, accepting Hess's offer of a beer. He sipped the Lucky Lager as Gloria's father paced back and forth in front of the bay window.

"Sounds like we may have a promising lead, Mr. Hess," the detective reassured the nervous father. "I'm meeting the guy tomorrow at eleven AM in Venice. I'll be carrying two hundred to give him if it's legit. After we meet, and once he takes me to where Gloria is supposedly working, I'll know if it is really her or not. Let's hope it is. Stay near your phone at work between eleven AM and one, so I can call you there."

"I'm not a religious person, but I pray to God it is her and we can end this search for my Gloria," sighed Mr. Hess.

"I hope you'll be able to talk to your daughter on the phone tomorrow, if all goes well. If it's a case of misidentification, or a scam, I'll know right away."

Lund finished his beer and set it on the coffee table. "I am heading home now, Mr. Hess. No point in continuing the search if we've really found her. I'll call you tomorrow, as promised, with the news—good or bad. Keep your fingers crossed and say a prayer to your god," said Steve. He shook Hess's sweaty hand and left for home.

The rookie detective called Uncle Bert again to make sure the plans for tomorrow's meeting were sound. Uncle Bert thought Steve's plan was solid but counseled Steve to make sure the meeting was with only one person in a location that looked safe, and keep a sharp eye out for guys loitering about near the appointed corner.

Steve left home the next morning at ten and drove to the designated intersection of Venice Boulevard and Pacific Avenue. He was about ten minutes early. He parked the Ford and ambled over to the southeast corner where a seedy liquor store was located. Steve bought a White Owl Panatela and stood at the store entrance, scanning the intersection area. He recognized the old guy who tottered up to the corner across the street as the old vag he had seen in the Venice alleyway; he still reminded Steve of the sad clown Emmett Kelly. The detective crossed the street and walked up to his man. "I'm Steve Lund. We meet again. You are the one with the information on Gloria Hess, aren't you?"

"I'm your man. Elmer Norton," the old bum replied, revealing a bad case of halitosis. "You got the two hundred with you?"

"I have your two hundred dollars right here, Mr. Norton," the detective stated as he discreetly flashed his stack of twenties.

"Let's go then," the old rummy demanded.

"My truck's across the street. You can give me directions on the way to where Gloria Hess works. I'll pay you the two hundred when I see that it is actually Gloria, not before, OK?"

"I hope you are an honest young man and not planning to cheat me," the stumblebum whined when he slowly climbed into Steve's panel truck. They headed north on Lincoln Boulevard towards Santa Monica. Steve was instructed to park near the Olympic Diner. They got out and walked to the diner, stopping just outside the dining-area windows on Olympic Boulevard.

"See, there she is! Right inside, waiting on that table, just like I said," the old drifter exclaimed excitedly. "Didn't I tell you on the phone I'd spotted your missing girl, Gloria Hess?"

"She sure resembles Gloria from out here, even with her hair bobbed and bleached," Steve agreed.

"Give me the two hundred and when do I get the rest of my money?"

"I think you're right, but I'm going inside and make sure it really is Gloria. You wait out here and stay put, and then I'll come out and pay you. I don't want her to panic and try to run. Don't go anywhere."

"You bet I won't," nodded the tramp.

Steve slipped inside the diner, sauntered over to the far end, and sat down at the counter a few stools away from the rest of the early-lunch customers. The young, blond waitress was busy with an order and did not recognize Steve until she stopped in front of him a few minutes later, pot of coffee in hand and ready to take his lunch order. Her eyes suddenly got big and her mouth opened but no sound came out.

An easy smile came over the detective's face. "Olly, Olly, Oxen Free, Glor. Time to come in. Game's over. I've done my part. Now it's your turn to act out the final scene of this charade. So far your father doesn't have a clue he is being snookered by his only daughter."

"Well, well! If it isn't good ol' Bloodhound Steve. How'd you pick up my scent?" the shocked young waitress exclaimed. Then she frowned. "Goddamn you, Lund. You weren't supposed to find me. I was supposed to contact you in four weeks, remember? That was the deal. So what happened? How'd you track me down so fast, anyway?"

"Purely an accident, Glor. Dumb luck, I guess. An old hobo spotted you in here from the flier I put out with your photo on it. He called your father about the reward money and asked for me. So I had no choice but to follow up his lead and play it straight. If your father had tracked down the old rummy himself, or found out somehow that I'd blown off a good lead, the whole scheme would have unraveled. Boom!" Steve's hand rose in the air for emphasis.

"And now what?" asked Gloria. "What about the reward money?"

"Think of the lost grand, the reward money, as a donation to charity. We still have five thou to split, three and two, with nobody the wiser. Tell your boss you need a break at two and we'll talk. Meanwhile, I'll have a burger basket and coffee, Blondie."

Steve left the diner and told anxious Elmer that it was indeed Gloria Hess, handing him ten new twenties. He promised to deliver the balance due of eight-hundred-dollars, tomorrow, right here, and even offered to buy him lunch at noon.

"How do I know you will show up?" asked the still-worried old man.

"Because I said I would. Besides, what choice do you have? Just be here tomorrow at noon. Don't blow your two hundred on a glorious bender and lose out on the other eight," admonished Steve.

The surfer detective went back into the diner for lunch and then made his call to the anxious father.

"It's her all right, Mr. Hess, your daughter, Gloria. The search is over quicker than we both expected and she's safe and sound. My uncle said she'd probably be in a populated beach area and his hunch paid off. I also got a bit lucky with a flier in the right hands. I'll have Gloria call you about two, so stay close to the phone. She can verify what I'm telling you."

"I had my doubts about you, Steve, but you came through for me. Thank you, thank you, thank you. You had never done anything like this before, and I really didn't know if you had the skills to track her down, but I was desperate, and you delivered. Thank god she is safe. Where is she?"

"I promised not to tell where she is. That was part of the agreement we had, remember? You wanted to know Gloria was OK and not in any trouble. I'm not a bounty hunter, hauling my prisoner back to the sheriff's office. You can talk to her this afternoon about coming home, but it's her decision. Keep that in mind. I'll see you tomorrow at ten, OK? You'll have to pay off the old guy who found Gloria and settle up with me for the five thousand due. If you can get my cashier's check and the old man's cash today, I'll meet you at your house at ten tomorrow morning."

"Steve, are you absolutely sure we have to pay that old drunk a thousand dollars just for spotting her? How about five hundred; I'm sure he'll settle for that. After all, he'll only drink it up anyway."

"The deal was for a grand—no less. We're not going to weasel him out of it now. He spotted her, and I gave him my word, promised the eight hundred by tomorrow. No welshing on the finder's fee, OK?"

"OK. OK. It was just a thought, but you're right, I suppose, that's the honorable thing to do. I'll have both your check and his money ready by tomorrow morning. I'll be waiting at home today at two for Gloria's call. I'm taking the rest of today off. Thank you again, Steve, for your perseverance in searching for and finding Gloria."

Steve went back to his truck and listened to KRLA's jazz music—Chet Baker, Stan Getz, Miles Davis, Chico Hamilton—until two, and then strolled back to the Olympic Diner to meet with the elusive and metamorphosed Gloria Hess.

They sat down at the back booth and Steve went over some hard and unpleasant facts. "This scam for your mom's life insurance money is a felony, you know. Plus, your fake disappearance act. Both of us could be wearing striped pajamas, doing hard time for this. Since you were a minor when your mother died, your father had the legal right to collect and pocket the six thousand. You knew that, even though your mother promised it to you and had named you her beneficiary."

"It's my money, Steve! My mother showed the policy to me before she died. She said it would be mine. He had no right to keep it. No right at all. He told me right after my mother's funeral, 'It doesn't matter, Gloria, that you were named on the policy. You are a minor and my money paid for the premiums.' That was bullshit!" said Gloria angrily. "My mom had some income of her own from a small family trust and she paid those premiums herself."

"Money does peculiar things to a person's thinking. It warps their personality so they can justify the rationalization of their selfish act. That alone doesn't make them totally bad. Your father does care for you. You know that. He was extremely upset and worried when you split. Your dad wouldn't have hired me to search for you and put up the reward money if he didn't give a shit what happened to you."

"I suppose you're right about that, but it still doesn't justify his keeping my money."

"Your three girlfriends were a big help to you. Hope they also know how to keep their mouths shut. They set your father up, just as you told them to, and fingered me as the guy for the bounty-hunter job. It amazes me that those three rattlebrains could keep their yaps zipped for this long. I hope to God you didn't mention the six-grand scam to any of them. All three would wet their panties over that. You didn't tell those airheads anything about the money, did you, Glor?"

"No. Not a word. They just knew I wanted to get away, that's all," she said.

"Your father did cough up the expenses and six grand for me to find you. It's not too late to bail out of this scheme, go home, and just forget the money."

"Are you kidding? I am not about to go back after being on my own, keeping my legs crossed like a good girl. I'll go to Santa Monica J.C. this fall too. The leash was too short and my collar too tight," she informed him. "You can tell my father that for me. When I was home, if my boyfriend wasn't the straight-arrow-looking type, studious, and preferably studying engineering, Dad would chase him off. I couldn't even talk to him about it. He has an Old World, German mentality. Everything had to be his way—always. Isn't it ironic he hired you, the typical surfer type, to look for me? He wouldn't have let your sort date me, day or night, not a chance in the world."

"Yeah, that doesn't surprise me, knowing him. I don't know that I'd want my daughter to date my sort either."

"I think his tight-ass mentality probably got to my mom and she literally blew a fuse. You know something? She had to smoke outdoors on the back porch, rain or shine, even in cold weather." Gloria lit up a Marlboro and exhaled a stream of smoke towards the diner's ceiling. "I'm not about to do that, no way.

"It's funny that he never had a clue that I was smoking too. Maybe he thought I loved the taste of Listerine, day and night. I was very careful not to burn holes in my clothes, otherwise they had to be given to the Salvation Army."

"We have to call your father now. You can tell him I found you and you're OK. Whatever else you say is up to you. I'm going to meet him tomorrow morning and pick up the five grand he owes me, plus the eight hundred for the old geezer," Steve told his blond bird in hand. "Just watch what you say to him. Don't screw this up now."

"Hello, Daddy, it's me. Your detective, Steve, found me... Yes, I'm fine. Listen to me, Dad, just listen for a minute. I had to get away from home to be on my own for a while. I didn't know any other way. There was no one I ran away with, no boyfriend, and no, I'm not pregnant. I just felt my chain was too short, so to speak. Where I am and what I'm doing suits me just fine for now, no telling for how long though," she informed her father.

"I want you to come home now, Gloria. This is a very foolish thing you are doing, and dangerous. Your foolishness is also going to cost me seven thousand dollars. Did you know that? SEVEN THOUSAND!" Dieter agonized.

"I guess you do owe Steve Lund that money for tracking me down. Sorry you had to go through an anxious time and that I cost you a ton of money. I was going to call you in a month and let you know I was safe. Let Steve pick up some clothes and personal things for me. I'll call you from time to time and talk, but for now let's just call this a consensual separation, OK?"

"No. It is not OK, Gloria. I want you to come home, today. This is your home, here. This nonsense of yours has to stop right now."

"I need time away and you can certainly get along without me for a while longer. I'll call you in a week and we can talk again. Meanwhile, pay Steve Lund what it is you owe him and give him some more of my things. That's the best way, the only way, for now at least. Now you know I'm all right and can make my own way, at least for the present. Get yourself a housekeeper, some German lady, to cook and keep house. Don't try to find me again. Your young detective got lucky. I'll let you know if anything happens, but I don't think it will. If you force the issue, it will only make the separation deeper between us. Now there's a bridge over it so don't burn it, will you, Dad?"

"You don't give me any choice, do you, Gloria? Promise me that you will call me in a few days and anytime you are having any difficulty."

"You have my word, Dad. I have to go back to work now. I'll call you soon," she responded with sadness in her voice as she hung up the phone.

"You did just fine, Glor," said Steve. "I'll see you here tomorrow with your stuff and the cash. Since you get off work at three, I'll meet you then. Wish me luck that tomorrow goes without any hitch."

"You should have no trouble carrying off our little scam, Steve. You're a natural smoothie," said a teary Gloria Hess, girl found.

Steve arrived at the Hess residence promptly at ten the next morning after sleeping a guiltless sleep at home until nine. Dieter Hess was in an unfathomable mood, in a muddle by dint of elation over the fact his daughter was found and despondency over the realization that she was not coming home—and that he was out seven thousand dollars.

"I'll absorb the two hundred advance paid to our lucky finder out of the advance you gave me and cut my employment time to three weeks at two hundred per week. You can write your personal check to me for six hundred and that will make us even for salary and expenses. Do you have the cashier's check for five grand and the eight hundred in cash?"

"Yes. Here they are, as you demanded. Gloria's things are in those two suitcases in the hall. If she needs anything else, she can call me," said Hess in a low voice. "Thank you for your help in finding my daughter. I just wish you could talk her into coming home."

"I think relations with your daughter will improve once you give her some time and show some patience. Maybe you could meet her somewhere for dinner soon, how's that sound?"

"I'd like that. Please tell her that I'd like that very much."

"You'd better call the Long Beach PD and tell them your daughter has been found and is safe. I wouldn't go into any details. They weren't of any help at all, anyway. By the way, most surfers are in fact anarchists and hedonists as you said when we first met on the beach at Huntington. The former proposes rejection of all forms of coercive control and authority, the latter pursuit of pleasure and avoidance of pain. You're probably not a disciple of either one, but I certainly am. Goodbye, Mr. Hess, I hope things turn out well in the end between you and Gloria," said the ex-detective as he turned and picked up Gloria's suitcases in the hallway.

Steve cashed the five thousand at his bank in Lakewood and put two grand of it in his checking account. The other three thousand he made into a new cashier's check payable to Gloria Hess.

All that cash in the hands of the old rummy probably wouldn't last a week, but there was also the possibility the thousand might extricate the old sod from the gutter. He called the manager of the YMCA in Santa Monica, who said over the phone that he would be willing to put up the old guy and dole out a few bucks a day to him. He also promised a part-time janitor job if Elmer wanted it. The allowance and the room and board would stretch for about two months. Enough time for the old bird to dry out and fly again, if he could tough it out. It was up to Elmer Norton to grab his last life ring and save himself from drowning in beer suds.

Since the ex-detective was headed for Santa Monica anyway, he thought he might as well stop on the way at the Velzy and Jacobs Surf Shop in Venice and order that hot new stick from Dale. After meeting with Gloria, he'd head on to Malibu for a few days of surfing and some "riding lessons" from Deloris.

Might as well let Bill Bristow finish out the thirty days on my NQA route and take some R and R for myself, Steve mused. If he pans out and doesn't fuck up or rip me off, maybe he would be interested in a sixty-forty split in nights and cash. No need for me to keep working six and seven nights anyway. I'll call Bettie and see what she thinks of him. I owe her a Franklin right about now, too!

I can pick up my new Velzy and hustle back to Long Beach and down to Huntington at the end of the week. In six days it'll be Golf Sunday. Roxanne should have the coffee and those buns hot and ready, thought Steve.

Then, I'll rent a new red Ford ragtop, buy myself some nice threads, and play "chase the fox" with the lady shrink. I know—we'll cruise over to the Lighthouse in Hermosa Beach for an evening. The Lighthouse, the premier jazz club on the West Coast, was always crowded from 9 PM to 2 AM and often even later, and smoky from grass, and filled with a diverse and hip clientele. Jerry Mulligan, who blows a very mean horn, was on the venue next week with his quintet. Cool jazz always puts a lady in a sexy mood, daydreamed the tanned waterman, two grand burning a hole in his hip pocket.

Epilogue
Ninety Days Later

"Detective Barnwell, Long Beach Police Department," said the heavy-set guy looking very out of place on the hot beach at Huntington in his rumpled blue serge suit, white dress shirt, and black brogans.

"I have a warrant for your arrest, Steven R. Lund, which reads 'Embezzlement of Funds.' That's a felony charge. Seems you fleeced someone's daddy out of seven grand in a phony missing girl scam this past summer. Ring a bell? Get up! I'm hauling your sandy ass back to Long Beach for trial. Your surfing days are over and washed up for a few good years, Lund." The pudgy cop grinned with look of satisfaction on his ruddy face.

"You have it all wrong, but I know it won't do any good to argue my case here on the beach. Right, detective? OK, I'll go with you—no fuss. Just let me wash the sand off my board and carry it up to the street to lock in my truck before we go. Can't just leave it here on the beach to get stolen.

You can cuff me there, if you want. Trust me, I'm not going to race off down the beach or put up a struggle and get shot in the chest—no way," assured Steve.

The arrestee, Steven R. Lund, slowly rose to his feet, picked up his Velzy, and balanced his board on his head. Detective Barnwell just stood there, nodded his head in acceptance, but unsnapped the holster holding the .38 Police Special strapped on his right hip.

Steve walked slowly down to the shoreline and slipped the surfboard into the shallow surf, giving it a little shove. He started splashing water on the top of the board and edged into waist-deep water, still throwing water topside.

"Far enough, Lund!" shouted the detective, now looking anxious as he stood at the surf line, trying to keep his shiny black brogans from getting wet.

"Just finishing up!" yelled Steve over his shoulder, as he gave the Velzy a hard shove seaward, slid onto the board, and began to paddle easily and outbound into deeper water and towards the breaker line. The detective at the shore pulled his revolver and yelled, "Get back here, Lund!" He aimed the .38 revolver seaward towards the escapee but didn't fire.

"Come back here!" the agitated detective shouted again and again. Steve kept stroking strongly, without looking back, out past the breaker line and towards the end of the Huntington Pier. The Newport Beach Pier was only five miles south. It would take over an hour of hard and steady paddling offshore to reach there. The odds that the Coast Guard or Newport Harbor patrol boat could be alerted and catch him just offshore within that time were remote, thought Steve, as he now continued to stroke southward.

He could hang out at Kenny E's Balboa pad for a week or two until the hunt for him cooled off. Estep could sneak back to Steve's pad and into his garage to pick up the stash of grass and two grand of cash Steve had hidden under the workbench. Two hundred and some grass for Kenny's risky work would do.

Then it would be time to search out an oceangoing sailboat in Newport Harbor that was headed for Hawaii and needed another deckhand. If that idea didn't pan out, he could hop a freighter out of San Diego. Quicksilver would have to wait a few more weeks for shipment to the Islands where NQA Messenger could resurface on Oahu. That was the plan for now.

Aloha

About the author

In 1938, aboard a tandem homemade paddleboard in Long Beach, at age six, Frank Warren had his first salty taste of surfing. It was the beginning of a lifelong love of the ocean waves.

Bodysurfing at Laguna Beach and Huntington Beach in the late 1940s led to longboarding on a used Hobie pigboard during the mid-1950s. San Onofre and Huntington Beach were Frank's and his buddies' main surfing venues those days. He is still bodysurfing and bellyboarding at his favorite spots on the North Shore of Oahu and Maui, at the age of eighty-four. Never too old to hit the waves for a cool ride.

The author in 1957